SYLVIA SMITH-SMITH

PETER NELSON

AN ARCHWAY PAPERBACK
Published by POCKET BOOKS

New York   London   Toronto   Sydney   Tokyo   Singapore

This book is a work of fiction. Names, characters, places and
incidents are either products of the author's imagination or are used
fictitiously. Any resemblance to actual events or locales or persons,
living or dead, is entirely coincidental.

Portions of the material in this book appeared in different form
in *Seventeen* magazine.

AN ARCHWAY PAPERBACK *Original*

An Archway Paperback published by
POCKET BOOKS, a division of Simon & Schuster Inc.
1230 Avenue of the Americas, New York, NY 10020

ISBN: 0-671-70586-5

First Archway Paperback printing April 1993

10 9 8 7 6 5 4 3 2 1

AN ARCHWAY PAPERBACK and colophon are
registered trademarks of Simon & Schuster Inc.

Cover photo by Michel LeGrou/Media Photo Group

Printed in the U.S.A.

IL 7+

For Ashley and A.J.

Contents

Sylvia Goes to the Prom

Proms are stupid. Proms are dumb. A waste of time and money, an archaic ritual dating back to the fifties, a costume party that won't admit it; a foolish fashion show where everybody gets snazzed up and then stands around in a tackily decorated ballroom, listening to a bad rock band play inept music so loud you can't even hear the nasty comments everybody makes behind the back of everybody else; the crowd subdividing into cliques, gear-heads in one corner, hackers in another, jocks here, punks there, preppies wearing Mom's pearls or Dad's cuff links and the Art Club kids dancing with their arms up in the air; and afterward the party in the house of whoever's parents are gone where you have three choices, make out, drink until you're sick, or both. The very idea almost made Sylvia nauseous.

So why did she want to go so much?

Because circumstances beyond her control—including difficult not-to-say-neurotic mothers who couldn't get along with workaholic not-to-say insecure fathers but not to name names—had forced her to grow up faster than she would have, had she been allowed to grow up in a normal family, in an ordered universe. She felt, in short, that her youth was passing her by.

"I *should* go to the prom," she told her dog, an old golden retriever named Betsy. "Even if I can't stand it and want to die. I'm young."

She ate a handful of popcorn and faced her second decision. Two boys had asked her, and she had to pick up the phone and say yes to one of them, tonight.

Stephen Field was nice, bright, honest and, above all else, short. Below all else? Sylvia had had numerous battles with him in government class. He was president of the school's Young Democrats Club, a real go-getter, nobody's all-time Mr. Handsome, but a good fellow, and she had such fun baiting him, advocating whatever opinion was opposite his, until he got all worked up arguing and his big ears turned red. A date with him was guaranteed to be lively. But . . . he had big ears that turned red. And she'd noticed a pimple on the end of his nose starting, which was sure to be huge and bulbous by prom time, only a week away. And the height difference—what if they got pulled over by the police, and Stephen, not quite a legal midget, got arrested for being an *illegal* midget?

Or David Rowan. Definitely taller than Stephen. Sylvia sat in front of him in German class. In fact, he'd asked her to go to the prom in German.

"Möchtest du mit mir zum der Schuletanzen gegehen?" he'd said.

2

"Willst du mit mir zum Abschlussfeier gehen?" she corrected him.

"Okay. When do I pick you up?"

He was funny, a decent dresser, a good student, nice looking, sort of sandy-haired and earnest, with a big natural smile. He could have been real popular if he'd wanted to be. That was the only problem— nobody really knew very much about him, and he kept to himself, without too many friends, if any. Sylvia was only half sure she wanted to know why that was. And why had he asked *her?* They were friends, but she hadn't even so much as dated him once, and the prom was supposed to be more than just a date.

Or she could just stay home.

"Sylvia," her mother called out just then. "Will you come here and help me put stamps on these envelopes? I'm all out of saliva."

No, Sylvia thought, I can't stay home.

"I'm on the phone, Mom," she called back. She picked it up and dialed. "Hello, David?" she began.

She sat in the front seat of David's car, trying not to jump to conclusions. So what if it were the most beat-up station wagon she'd ever seen, and she had to get in the driver's side and slide over because the passenger's side door had been lashed shut ever since David had backed into a telephone pole with the door open when a girl named Anita had forgotten to close it two years ago. And so what if it smelled like turpentine, in spite of (or because of?) a deodorizer in the shape of a Smurf, hanging from the rearview mirror?

"All you have to do is this," David said. He patted the dashboard affectionately. "Good car. Now *you* do it."

"Good car," Sylvia said, patting the dash.

"Very low maintenance," David said. "One pat every five miles and the car is fine."

He looked, Sylvia thought, sensational, a basic black tuxedo, none of the goofy pastel blues and greens she knew other boys would be wearing—he had taste, in tuxes, if not in flowers. She gave him a red carnation and he gave her a corsage the size of a juniper bush.

"It's beautiful," she said. So she'd rot in hell for lying.

"Want me to pin it on you?"

"Oh, uh, no," she said. "I can't have it near my face. Uh, allergies. I'll just hold it." And then bury it in the lettuce when I get to the salad bar.

"It is kind of stupid," he said, "to hang an ugly old orchid on someone as pretty as you are tonight."

"Smile, you two," Sylvia's mother said, pointing the camera at them. Sylvia hoped her blushing wouldn't show. No one had ever paid her a compliment like that.

After she took their picture her mother had them take one of her, for posterity.

"Your mother is quite unique," was David's comment.

"You mean strange?" Sylvia said.

"Unregalmässig," he said.

"Irregular," Sylvia agreed. "I thought you didn't know irregular verbs?"

"Is that what *unregalmässig* means?" She laughed.

4

There was something about him, so casual and confident, so . . . she couldn't find the word. Mature? Wise?

And then at dinner. They'd decided to do it up right, shoot the traditional works, tuxes, gowns, flowers, dinner—dutch, of course. At dinner she noticed it again. Instead of trying to impress her, for the most part, he just sat there asking her questions, listening to her answers. Sylvia noticed another group of kids from her school in the same restaurant, three girls and their dates, and the boys were being so obnoxious, loud and probably drunk or stoned, trying to impress, that the maitre d' had to come over and ask them to pipe down. It embarrassed Sylvia, and she wasn't even with them. Sylvia told David all about growing up, her old neighborhood, the old house, the problems her parents had had, how she felt when her dad moved out, or when she and her mom moved into the new place. Sylvia talked the whole time, feeling perfectly at ease, enjoying David's company.

So she sat in the car, trying not to jump to conclusions. So, so what if she felt so terrific? It didn't necessarily mean she was falling in love. Did it? How could it?

Who, her?

She was so confused.

They danced the first five dances, nonstop, and then found a table to sit at. David was a surprisingly good dancer and made Sylvia feel far less awkward than she usually felt. The prom was pretty much what Sylvia had expected, everyone playing dress-up, girls in backless gowns with elbow-length gloves and the whole rigmarole, but it was all good fun. Sylvia wore a simple black dress, white stockings and bright red shoes to match a bright red silk scarf her mother had given her. Everyone thought she looked hot, in a French sort of way. Her friend Marcie told her, when David was out of earshot getting refreshments, that she couldn't believe how handsome David was, the two of them easily in the running for the handsomest couple.

"Oh pull-ease, Marcie, if you nominate us, I'll kill you, swear to God."

"Too late," Marcie said. "It's true, though. Are you sure that's the same David Rowan?"

"How would I know?" Sylvia said.

"What?" Marcie said. It suddenly occurred to Sylvia that, for all the talking they'd done already that night, she still knew next to nothing about him, almost like he was hiding something, not really shy, more like . . . what? Secretive?

"I just mean we're still getting to know each other, that's all," she said.

"Well if you *really* want to get to know each other, there's a party at Bobby Templeton's house afterward. His mom's in Florida."

When David returned, Sylvia suggested they find a quiet place away from the music. On their way they passed Mr. Potter, the school guidance counselor, and Sylvia smiled at him. They'd had more than one good talk in their day, and Sylvia knew she'd miss him after she graduated. They found a circular booth in the corner.

"I feel so sorry for him, standing there all alone," Sylvia said. "His wife died two years ago."

"Uh-huh," David said. "So tell me, why'd you bring me to this dark corner? You're not going to try anything, are you?"

"Maybe I am, maybe not," she said. "Actually, you can trust me—I have a good head on my shoulders. My mother says so all the time."

"I like your mother," he said. "Tell me about your father."

"Well, he's—" Sylvia began, catching herself. "No. You always do that, and I've been talking about myself all night. You tell me about you for a change."

"I'm a spy. That's all I'm allowed to say."

"David . . ."

"I'm from the future, and I've come back to prevent World War III. Done a pretty good job, too, so far, don't you think?"

"Be serious."

"That's not serious?" he said.

"Stop it," she said. "No more kidding. I realized I don't know anything about you. Here I like you, and I don't even know who you are. Where do you go after school? Where do you live, geez, I don't even . . ."

"You like me?"

"Sure," she said. He slid next to her on the booth. "Don't evade the question."

"Maybe I don't like to talk about myself," he said. "What I do like is you, very very very much, Sylvia Smith-Smith-Smith."

"Just two Smiths," she said. Their faces were only eight inches apart. He had the biggest brown eyes she'd ever seen.

"Now," he said, "beautiful, brilliant sexy Sylvia, if you had a choice between talking or kissing, which would you rather do?" He moved beside her and put his arms around her.

"You mean here?" she said.

"Here."

"Now?"

"Right now."

"Talk," she said. He kissed her. She closed her eyes and enjoyed it. "Kissing's okay too, though," she whispered.

She could not believe she was making out in the corner at the prom. It was just perfect. She'd wanted to do the things you do when you're young, so she let herself, and was not embarrassed—in fact, when a kiss broke off, it was more often she than David who began the next one, and every kiss was different from the one before it, like songs on the radio, hit after hit. Mostly she kept her eyes closed, but when she did open them, she saw the mirrored prom ball throwing streamers of lights around the room and the decorations sparkling, the people moving to the music, and somehow it wasn't corny anymore. Vaguely she wondered what it was she was supposed to do next, and why she was kissing him at all—why did people kiss? But only vaguely, and never for long.

"Wow," he said at last.

"Wow," she said.

"Sylvia," he said, "there is something I have to tell you."

"What?"

"I hope you won't mind," he said, "but I've got to go to the bathroom."

In his absence, Sylvia calmed down, gathered her wits, still glowing with the warmth of the moment. On the stage, the health teacher, Mr. Rodriguez, the most popular teacher in school, was organizing a snowball dance, starting with the king and queen of the prom. It was outrageously queer, but Sylvia wanted to be part of it. Mr. Potter was still standing where she'd seen him last, hands clasped behind his back. Sylvia tiptoed up to him and tapped him on the shoulder.

"Hey, mister chaperon," Sylvia said. "Wanna dance with your favorite brat?"

"Sylvia," he said, singing out her name. "You look beautiful. Thank you, but I really wouldn't begin to know how. The last dance I ever did was the twist."

"That's okay," she said.

"Are you having a good time?"

"I'm having a *great* time," she said, shouting to be heard over the music. "I can't believe it. I thought I'd hate it, but I love it."

"Was that David Rowan I saw you with?" he asked.

"Yeah," Sylvia said. "Ain't he just cool?"

"Sylvia," he said. There was a look of concern on his face.

"What?" she said. He was struggling to say something. "What is it?"

"You know that the things you and I talk about when you come into my office are confidential, don't you?" he said. She nodded. "There are things I'm not at liberty to discuss, and I know I really shouldn't say anything, but . . ."

"But what?"

"Just be careful, that's all."

"Be careful?"

"Yes," he said. "With David, I mean."

* * *

"You want to tell me what's wrong?" David said. They were parked in front of Bobby Templeton's house. They could hear the party from the street. Sylvia wished her door opened—she felt trapped with it wired shut. "If you don't want to go to the party, we don't have to."

"I want to," she said. "Let's go." He got out and let her sidle past him. She walked up the steps, and heard David talking to himself, but loud enough for her to hear, saying, "This is crazy. One minute she likes me, the next minute she treats me like I have the plague."

Sylvia headed straight for the kitchen. She was relieved to see Stephen Field standing by the refrigerator.

"Hey, Communist," Sylvia said to him. "You here infiltrating by yourself, or do you have a date?"

"Hi, Sylvia," he said. "I'm here with Nancy Byers, but I don't know where she went." The house was crowded, forty or fifty kids altogether.

"Maybe she ditched you," Sylvia said.

"Maybe she did," he said. "Maybe I ditched her."

"It's good to see you having fun, anyway," Sylvia said. "I suppose this means that you agree with President Reagan that America is back and it's time to feel good again?"

"Don't start with me," he said. "What the student council spent on decorations alone could feed a hundred Ethiopians for a year."

"So let them cancel their own proms," Sylvia said. "Just kidding." She felt a hand on her elbow. It was David.

"Could I have a word with you?" he whispered in her ear. She followed him into the hall.

"What's going on?" he asked.

"What do you mean?" she said.

"I mean one minute you're kissing me and then as soon as we get here, you start to ignore me completely."

"Don't be so sensitive. I wasn't ignoring you, David," she said. "I was talking to my friend Stephen. That *is* what parties are for, is it not? You move around, meet people, mingle and talk. If you don't want to do that, why go to a party in the first place?"

"Oh stop it," David said, looking her in the eye.

There it was again, the feeling Sylvia had with David, that he understood her, or could see through her somehow. That she couldn't fool him.

"If you don't want to tell me what's making you so weird, then fine. I met your mother, so I guess there's a certain amount of that in your family, but if you don't want to talk to me, then I'd just as soon go home, because I can tell right now I'm not going to have any fun here."

"Wait," Sylvia said. After Mr. Potter's warning, she'd decided to simply play the night out, cut her losses and go home, but she could see that wasn't going to work. And she felt she owed him something. "Okay," she said, "but not here. Someplace private." There was a stairway leading down into the basement, and they descended it. There were noises off to the right, people in a room doing God only knows what, so she turned left, opening the first door she came to. The room was windowless, pitch-black, and the switch on the wall didn't work, but enough light shone through the open door for her to see the shape of a couch, in what looked like some sort of den or study.

11

She went and sat on the couch. When David closed the door behind him, it was so dark she couldn't see her hand, three inches from her face.

"I'm surprised you trust me enough to sit in a dark room with me," he said. She clapped her hands once. "What was that?"

"They say that blind people can tell how big a room is just by clapping their hands," she said.

"So how big is it?"

"Not so big," she said. "I'm sorry David. I probably have been acting weird, and I apologize. Just don't compare me to my mother again."

"Oh," he said. "It's okay. I just don't understand why you liked me at first and now you don't."

"It isn't that I don't," she said, "It's just . . . oh God, I don't exactly know, either. Okay. A friend of mine, who I trust, told me to be careful with you."

"Who?"

"I can't tell you," she said. "It just scared me."

"Why?"

"Why do you think?" Sylvia said. "Maybe because it occurred to me that for all I know, you could be a drug dealer or something."

"What?" he said. "Have you ever seen anybody making all that money dealing dope who drives a car like I have?"

"That also occurred to me," she said. "Maybe it's because I found myself developing a big crush on you, and then I realized that you've told me so little about yourself that I have good reason to be careful because you act like you're hiding something."

"You're so smart," David said. *"Und auch so schön.* I can't stand it."

"So?" she said. There was a long pause.

"So okay. Ask me anything," he said. "Total honesty, I promise."

It was still too dark to see anything. She felt like they were two people in a mine, trapped by a cave-in, waiting for rescue, talking to keep from being afraid. She could hear the music through the floor, and the rumble people dancing made sounded like thunder.

"Where do you live?" she asked.

"1143 Burke Street. Apartment 3G."

"Good," Sylvia said. "Was that so hard?"

"No," he said.

"Where do you go every day, after school, when the rest of us are just hanging out?"

"1143 Burke Street."

"Apartment 3G."

"Actually, all of them," he said. "There are sixteen units, and I take care of the building and do maintenance in all the apartments. I'm usually working from after school until nine or ten at night. Which is why I never have time to study and never learned my *unregalmässig* verbs."

"So you have a job then," Sylvia said. "Why was that so hard to tell me? Lots of people have jobs."

"It's not exactly a job," David said. "I own the building."

"What?" Sylvia said. She was shocked. She edged away from him on the couch. "How old *are* you?"

"Eighteen," he said. "I missed a year. Why, how old are you?"

"Seventeen," she said. "How can anybody own a building when he's eighteen? Isn't that illegal or something?"

"I inherited it when my dad died, four years ago. He had kidney failure."

"Oh God," Sylvia said. "I'm so sorry." She slid toward him, and put her hand on his.

"It's okay," he said. "He was sick a long time, so it wasn't unexpected. It's not like I mean to hide it. I just don't bring it up if I don't have to."

"So you live with your mother then?" she asked. "Brothers? Sisters?"

"None on either count," he said. "And I don't live with my mother." Sylvia heard a big sigh. "My mother got remarried, to a guy I think she was seeing before my dad died. Of course, she waited six months to make it look good."

"Oh no," Sylvia said. She wished she could see David's face. " 'An act that blurs the grace and blush of modesty.' "

"What?" he said.

"I played Gertrude last year when the school did *Hamlet*," Sylvia said. "That's what Hamlet says to his mother, when she gets married again a month after his father dies. My parents were splitting up at the time. It was so bad they couldn't even stand to come to the same performance, and I kept thinking of those lines. Shakespeare says it 'takes off the rose from the fair forehead of an innocent love and sets it a blister there, makes marriage vows as false as dicers' oaths.' A dicer is a crapshooter."

"It's true," David said. "Geez, I always wondered why Shakespeare was so good, but now he's bumming me out, five hundred years after he's been dead. I should read *Hamlet*."

"More like 350 years," Sylvia said, "but yeah, you should. You live alone then? Don't you get lonely?"

"I can't see you," David said. "Are you sitting down, because you should be. You asked for total honesty, right?"

"Right."

"No, I don't live alone."

"Who with then?"

"You remember Anita? The girl I told you forgot to shut the passenger side door, so I backed up and bent it?"

"You live with her?"

"Yeah," David said. "I broke the door the night she told me she was pregnant. Sylvia, I'm married, and I have a two-and-a-half-year-old son named Josh."

"Oh get out of here," Sylvia said. She waited for the words, "Just kidding." They didn't come.

The silence in the room was deafening.

"Oh no," Sylvia said. "I don't believe this. I'm seventeen years old, and I'm having an affair with a married man."

"You want me to explain?" David asked. Sylvia said yes, maybe he'd better.

It was not a happy story. After his father's death, when it became clear that his mother was going to hastily remarry, David lost control of the better parts of himself—he could see no good reason not to. Fate had dealt him the proverbial cruel blow, and he did the best he could to deny and resist it, unaware that resisting fate was impossible. He quit school, the year he'd told Sylvia he'd missed, refused to listen or do anything about the complaints of the tenants, fought with his mother and mostly stayed home during the days, drinking. At night he'd go out, often not returning until the following morning, cruising the streets, getting in trouble. One of those nights he spent with Anita, a girl he'd seen only a few times before, and that night he made her pregnant. When she told him she was going to have it, he felt he had only two choices, one to shape up and "do the honorable thing," the other to let go, give up, bottom out, go the way he'd seen other kids go, the ones who were always on the edges and margins of everything, leaning in corners or sitting alone in their cars smoking cigarettes, until one day they'd just disappear without anybody ever wondering where they went or missing them because nobody'd ever known their names in the first place.

They got married, but even before Josh was born, both he and Anita knew they didn't love each other, and never would grow to love each other—it was simply as clearly true as the light of day. Now they continued to live together, to save money, but planned on getting divorced just as soon as they'd saved enough to pay the court costs and legal fees, no small amount these days. David intended to give Anita a free apartment, as soon as one opened up, but she was going to trade school, had a semiserious boyfriend and didn't mind David going out with Sylvia in the least. Both Anita and David loved Josh with all their hearts and would take care of him, but as far as the marriage went, that was a big mistake.

"Well," David said, when he was done. "You hate my guts with a shovel, right? I mean, this ruins it, right?"

16

"No," Sylvia said. "It changes it, but it doesn't have to ruin it, I don't think." There was no word to describe the way she felt. A loud, formless scream might come close. "All I wanted was to go to the prom like a normal kid—was that too much to ask?"

"All *you* wanted?" David said. He laughed. "What about me? I make one colossal stupid mistake when I'm fifteen and find myself a married father with an apartment building to take care of. I didn't want to bring any of this up." Sylvia started to giggle. "Boys just want to have fun too, you know. What's so funny?"

"It's just so funny," she said. "I can just see your wife, waiting up with a rolling pin saying, 'Don't lie to me, Ralph Kramden, I know where you've been—you've been to the *prom*, haven't you?'" Now they both laughed, and kept on laughing.

"Oh geez," David said, catching his breath. "So we can be friends, then?"

"Sure," Sylvia said, "but just friends. I can't handle the rest of it."

"Me, either," he said. "I just wanted to go to the prom like everybody else, really."

"Well, let's boogie on upstairs and get dancing," Sylvia said. "The night is still young. It isn't a prom unless you stay out too late and get yelled at by your folks. Or your wife!" she said, cracking up all over again.

They kissed one last time, briefly, and left. At the foot of the stairs, Sylvia remembered she'd kicked off her shoes while they were talking and had left them behind. She went back for them but couldn't locate them. She groped in the dark until she found a desk.

There was a fluorescent lamp on it, and she turned it on. She then saw, across the room from the couch she and David had sat on, a second couch, and seated there, Stephen and Marcie.

"You rats!" Sylvia said. "How long were you listening?"

"Oh God, Sylvia, we're so sorry. We were going to tell you, then we were waiting for the right moment and then we couldn't because—"

"Marcie," Sylvia said, "so help me, if you breathe so much as a word of this to anyone, I'll tell everyone in school that you wear eight pairs of underpants at the same time so it'll look like you have hips."

"You wouldn't," Marcie said.

"You do?" Stephen said.

"And as for you, Stephen Field, you tiny little man," Sylvia said, "if you say anything at all, I will be delighted to personally see to it that your name gets on the mailing list of every crackpot conservative group in this country, including the KKK and the National Rifle Association."

"You wouldn't."

"Try me."

"I promise," he said.

"Okay," she said. "Now we're all going to go upstairs, and we're going to have fun, because this is the prom, right?"

"Right," they said.

"Now move it," she commanded. "Hey, wait a minute! Didn't you both come with other people?"

"We promise, Sylvia," Marcie said, "not a word. Deal?"

On her way up the stairs, Sylvia tried to decide if

she felt more happy or sad. She knew her heart entertained huge amounts of both feelings, that she was feeling a little sorry for David and a little sorry for herself, but all in all, glad she hadn't stayed home, enriched by the entire, strange, eye-opening night.

> Proms are stupid.
> Proms are dumb.
> Life is a prom
> Oh won't you come?

One of her father's pet phrases occurred to her. "If you want to dance, you've got to pay the band." She made mental note that the next time he said that, she'd say, "Yeah, but if you've already paid the band, you might as well dance."

Meet Sylvia Smith-Smith

Urgent! Urgent! Wake up the president. The Earth is about to collide with the sun!"

"Gentlemen, gentlemen, let him sleep—he couldn't handle this anyway. This looks like a job for . . . Sylvia Smith-Smith!"

"But general, she's only a teenager."

"Yes, but she's got a good head on her shoulders."

Sylvia stood in a long line at the bank, admiring the head on her shoulders in the wall mirror. It was true. Her head was exactly where it was supposed to be, pointing in the right direction, securely in place, with a plain but not unattractive face on the front of it, light brown hair everywhere else, soft white stocking cap, scarf, glasses. She examined the heads of the twenty-six people in front of her, waiting to withdraw or deposit.

* * *

Suddenly, the wealthy international financier's head fell off, making a melonlike hollow thud as it bounced on the marble floor. Now he definitely had a bad head on his shoulders, Sylvia thought. Screams.

"Oh my God!" a woman said, a shoe clerk from Teaneck married to a hunchback. "His head fell off! I think I'm going to faint!"

"For pete's sake, somebody get a doctor," a man said.

Sylvia cleared her throat.

"Excuse me," she said, "I'm Sylvia Smith-Smith." Ooohs and aaahs. The crowd parted to let her through.

"What an extraordinarily fortunate coincidence that she's here," a man said, a CIA agent with microdots between his teeth. Sylvia picked up the financier's head and patted it gently.

"Don't worry," she said, "I'm Sylvia Smith-Smith, the most sensible person in this whole crazy world, according to my mother."

"Thank God," the financier's head said. Sylvia reached inside the man's skull and rotated the *pendulum obligato* a half turn clockwise. She took a syringe loaded with very expensive brain glue from her purse and applied it liberally to both surfaces, allowed fifteen seconds for drying, then stuck the man's head back on.

"How's that feel?"

"It feels great," he said, working his jaw, "better than before, even. Please allow me to bestow upon you valuable riches—a yacht, perhaps?"

"Oh no," she said humbly, "no thanks. Sylvia Smith-Smith asks for nothing in return."

She opened her bank book. She had $18,622 in her account. Not bad for a kid, except only $131 of it was hers. The rest belonged to her mother.

"Lord knows I should be explaining this to you, dear," her mother had said, "but until this whole thing is finished, I think the less I have in your father's and my account, the easier it will be, you know, to get at it . . . in case of emergencies. Just until the legal beagles have done with us, all right? Love? I wish I had a better head for money. You could probably invest it for me and double it."

"My broker says I should buy at twenty-four and a half and hope it splits at thirty, as long as the Dow holds even with the blue chips. What does your broker say?"

"Well, my broker is Sylvia Smith-Smith, and Sylvia Smith-Smith says . . ."

Everybody in line was staring at her, suddenly hushed.

"Sylvia," Mr. Potter, the school counselor had said, "how are things at home?"

She inched forward in the bank line.

"Which home?"

"Oh," Mr. Potter said, "I'm sorry. Let's see, when was the last time we—" shuffling papers "—ah. So, some time in the last month, your, ah, father . . ."

"My mother moved," Sylvia said.

"Your mother. I see. Do you live with your mother then? Is it a nice place?"

"It's okay," she said. "It's just an old house. The furnace shut down last weekend and we nearly froze, but I fixed it."

"You fixed the furnace?" he said. He pushed his glasses up the bridge of his nose and sniffed. "I wouldn't even know how to . . . I'd be afraid to blow up the house."

"It's not that complicated," she said, trying to keep the sarcasm out of her voice. "It was just the water. If the gauge says the boiler's empty, you have to turn a faucet on to fill it again, halfway, or it won't start."

"I suppose people tell you all the time what a remarkable girl you are, don't they?"

"You are a remarkable girl," the man in front of her said, with a slight accent, removing his ski mask to reveal a face halfway between Robert Redford and Magnum P.I. "Allow me to introduce myself. I am Sir Edmund Greycroft-Lancaster, duke of Marlboro, heir to the throne of Dolbania and also an extremely world-famous rock star. And you are?"

"Just a girl."

"Just a girl? Just a girl? Nay, the epitome of womanhood, an Egyptian queen, lunar goddess and dream girl of my life. Come with me to Dolbania . . . I will build you a castle out of diamonds and gold, and you can be the principal dancer in the Royale Ballet."

"Sorry, I have to go home after school and give my mom's car a tune-up. I'm a very responsible person, you know."

"But don't you understand?" he said. "I am dying.

To tell you the truth, I'm too handsome to live. Marry me, and after I'm dead, a month, three months, tops, I swear, you will be queen of Dolbania and have all the money in the known universe."

"That's awfully tempting, really, thanks, but no thanks. For you see, my sweet sweet prince, it's important at this point in our lives for us to be strong and independent, and learn not to be reliant on men, because some you can count on, but some you can't, and if one lets you down, even if he's your father, and you have nothing to fall back on, you're in deep dark waters, love. We will probably be surprised to learn the things we can do on our own, if we only try."

"Your name, then," the duke of Marlboro said, a single, golden tear on his cheek, "I beg you, at least tell me your name . . ."

Father's name, Smith.

Mother's maiden name, Smith.

Sylvia's mother refused to take her father's name, after the marriage.

"But my name *is* your name," he said.

"Your name is *your* name and *my* name is *my* name," she said. "Fini! The end. Oh don't ask me to make sense, love, because I don't want to make sense. I warned you I was stubborn, but that's why you love me, isn't it? Isn't it?"

Good marriages, Sylvia's common sense told her, employ a system of give and take. In her parent's case, something had short-circuited.

"Your mother's insane," Sylvia's best friend Marcie said.

"My mother is not insane."

"Oh come on, Sylvia, don't be so literal. I just mean she's so . . . unusual."

"Idiosyncratic," Sylvia said, "an 'excess unto herself,' my father always says."

"Bizarre."

"Oui, très bizarre, n'est-ce pas?"

"She's neat, though. I mean, I really like her."

"So do I," Sylvia said.

"Sylvia," Mr. Potter said, "you know, your mother and father are both lucky to have you."

"I know," she said. She didn't mind talking to Mr. Potter, but this was her study hall, and she still had a page on Nathaniel Hawthorne to write before fifth hour.

"You know, Sylvia, it's tough when people get divorced because it makes their kids grow up a lot faster than they would, ordinarily." Everyone seemed to be terribly fond of saying this.

"Maybe the court will give you custody of your parents," Marcie had joked, "then you can tell them if they don't get back together, they're grounded."

"It's okay," Sylvia told Mr. Potter, "really. Everybody's folks get divorced."

"Sometimes," Mr. Potter continued, "kids will try to keep their parents from separating by creating a bigger problem for them than the one, or rather I should say the ones that are keeping them from, uh, staying together."

"Really?" she said. "Does it work?"

"Sylvia, no," he said, pinching his big nose with a

handkerchief. "Listen. I mean, okay, for instance, a lot of girls might stop eating, or even, er, become . . ."

"Sexually active?"

"Well—"

"Mr. Potter, can I go please? I have a ton of work to do, and if that's all you want to know, really, everything's okay. I never even thought about creating problems, until now, anyway, and I have boys who are my friends but that's all, and I eat like a pig. No I don't, I just eat normal. I'm the one who has to be okay, because I'm the only way my parents talk to each other anymore, so there's nothing to worry about."

"Maybe I'm an old fuddy-duddy," he said, "but if it's all right with you, I'll just worry anyway. Okay?"

"Okay."

"If you ever need to talk, you know," he said.

"I know."

"I'll be happy to write you a pass. You can call me at home, too. Here." He wrote his telephone number on a slip of paper and handed it to her.

It took fifteen minutes for Sylvia to reach the front of the bank line. When she got there, she glanced left, then right, through narrowed eyes. She bet herself a dollar the first teller to open up would be the goodlooking black man, but drew a middle-aged woman with silver glasses instead. No matter. Sylvia put her heavy bag on the counter. The red passbook was at the top, with the slip of paper Mr. Potter had given her inside it. She closed her eyes, imagining tomorrow's headlines. She handed the teller a folded-up garbage bag, then took a .357 Magnum from her purse and pointed it at her.

"Freeze, turkey!" she said with a practiced authority, a sneer in her voice. "Put the money in the bag, and don't touch no buttons or I'll blow you away!"

That wasn't so hard. Now all she had to do was wait. Everything was going according to plan, and she'd planned carefully. She did, after all, have a good head on her shoulders.

"Miss? Can I help you? Miss?"
Sylvia reached into her purse.

Sylvia's Masquerade

What do you think?" Sylvia said to her friend Marcie. They stood before Sylvia's full-length mirror.

"Not enough," Marcie said. "You have to put it on so heavy that when you blink, you can *hear* your eyelashes clicking."

"Check!" Sylvia said. She imitated the voice fashion show emcees used. "Yvonne's exotic Mad Maxine motif is offset by the piquant sauciness of her black-and-white checkered mascara, rendering the effect bon vivant without diminishing its corpselike savoir faire."

The girls shrieked with laughter.

"Oh yes," Marcie said. "Do zebra stripes for me, Sylvia."

"Not Sylvia," Sylvia said, "Yvonne, like Yvonne DeCarlo, from *The Munsters.*"

"That's still too ordinary a name," Marcie said.

"What are you calling yourself?" Sylvia said.

"Pustule," Marcie said. Sylvia laughed.

"Furry Zygote, the Fiend from Hell!" Sylvia said.

"Puke Geyser, the Creature from Hoboken," Marcie said.

Sylvia looked at herself in the mirror. How do people live like this? She had on a tight black sleeveless top, tight black pants that stopped at midcalf, with the drive chain from a Harley-Davidson for a belt. She wore black biker boots with a pink-and-black scarf tied around her right ankle and a chain of broken beer-bottle necks around the left one. Safety pins held together the seam of her left pant leg, and she'd laced her right pant leg with bamboo shish kebab skewers until it bristled like a porcupine. No easy trick, she told Marcie, considering she'd have to sit down and/or dance in her getup, without acupuncturing herself to death. A complete and total trashing of her mother's scarf drawer had turned up a brown and black leopard bandanna, which Sylvia wore around her neck, in the front, as well as a tie-dyed khaki-colored neckerchief with navy blue peace signs on it, a relic from her mother's sixties college protest days, which Sylvia wore around her neck, in the back. Her face, of course, was done in the traditional punk two-tone, white Pan-Cake makeup with black eyeliner and lipstick. She had a rhinestone earring dangling from her left earlobe and a broken Lady Bulova hanging from the other, as well as assorted rings and clips up the helix. Marcie, who was planning to be an art major in college, had drawn India-ink tattoos on Sylvia's bare arms, a skull and crossbones on her left biceps, a heart with an arrow through it and the words Bob Newhart

—Forever! under it on her right biceps, even a ship's anchor and the words "S.S.Smith" on her forearm. Marcie was adorned similarly, but all of this was nothing compared to what they'd done to their hair. First, of course, they'd dyed it black, Marcie leaving a streak of her natural blond, using a hair coloring guaranteed to wash out, and just to be sure, Marcie had tested it on her little brother's hamster. Then Sylvia had a stroke of genius. Once the dye was dry, they went back to school, where Mr. Kerr, the physics teacher, let Sylvia and Marcie use the Van de Graaff generator. Sylvia put her hand on it, while Mr. Kerr turned the crank. The static electricity made Sylvia's hair stand straight out from her head in all directions. Marcie emptied an entire can of industrial-strength hair spray into Sylvia's mane, to freeze it in place, and then Sylvia did the same for Marcie. The results were spectacular—it made Tina Turner's fright wig look like a Princess Diana special. Both Marcie and Sylvia looked outstandingly disgustingly mega-ultra-radically punk, but then, that was the point. They were, after all, going to a Halloween party.

The doorbell rang, and Sylvia's mother called up the stairs that "someone or some*thing*" was there to pick them up. They made their entrance, walking down the steps like fashion models, sideways, one step at a time.

"Ladies and gentlemen," Sylvia said, "we present this year's line of evening wear, 'A Touch of Crass.' The new oh-so-très-bon-chic look that says look out world, we're going to make you sick."

"Oh Syl," her mother said, "you look so cute!"

"*Cute,* Mom?" Sylvia said. "We spend three hours making ourselves ugly, and you say we're cute?"

"Well," Sylvia's mother said, "in a revolting kind of way."

"That's better," Sylvia said.

"Are you supposed to be boys or girls?" her mother said. Sylvia slapped herself on the forehead in disbelief.

"Mother, please, *try* to get with it. We're androgynous, okay?"

"The rule at school," Marcie said, "is if you have to ask, it doesn't matter."

"This is Kathy," Sylvia said, introducing the also punked-out someone or something standing in the doorway. "She's driving."

"Pictures!" Sylvia's mother said.

"More pictures?" Sylvia said. She remembered the prom.

"Nobody move."

Marcie was planning to wear a long black cape. She put it on for the photo session.

"You're going to die in that thing," Sylvia said. "It's going to be hot on the dance floor."

"Gotta wear it, though," Marcie said. "Punks don't dress for comfort. They're too cynical to be comfortable."

"They're too stupid," Kathy said.

"They're too fried from drugs," Sylvia said. "They're like the bag people who wear winter coats in August—they've lost the ability to regulate their body temperature."

Sylvia's mother came downstairs carrying her camera and also, under one arm, a stuffed six-foot-long barracuda that she'd once caught in Florida. She told the girls to stand by the fireplace and hold the fish.

"You don't want this to be an ordinary picture, do you?" she said. "Ooh, you're all so *cute.*"

"Mom," Sylvia said, "we're not cute. We're toxic waste."

"Yeah, but you're my little toxic waste," her mother said. "Okay everybody, smile—say 'sleaze.'"

"SLEAZE!" the girls said.

The party, although it was being sponsored by Weston High School, under the theme "Any Witch Way You Want," was not being held at the school, which was having its gym floors refinished before basketball season started. Their destination was, instead, the Mennasett Beach Club, an old, sprawling stucco building, white with red trim, that was at one time part of a popular amusement park that had closed back in the fifties, though the merry-go-round was still operating. Sylvia, Marcie and Kathy were going to meet their other punked-out friends at the merry-go-round, which stayed open until the first week of November, and decide then whether to actually go to the dance or just hang out, whichever would allow them to be seen by the maximum number of people.

Were going to.

They were on the freeway when Kathy's father's Pontiac began inexplicably to lose power. Kathy stepped on the gas, but the car continued to slow, until she had to pull over onto the shoulder. The car was dead.

"Oh God," Kathy said, "my father's going to kill me."

"I'm going to kill you," Marcie said. "I don't believe this—the greatest party of the year, and we're going to miss it."

They got out to look under the hood. Marcie found a yellow flashlight in the glove compartment. The first car that passed them yelled something at them. Their engine was a fairly standard American V8, an immense mass of tubes, wires and mechanical shapes. Sylvia asked for the flashlight.

"Holy moly," Marcie said. "You'd have to be a professor at Harvard to understand this thing."

"Marcie," Sylvia said. "Ernie Pendergrass could take this apart with his eyes closed, and he's not exactly bright enough to be a professor at Harvard."

"He's barely bright enough to be Ernie Pendergrass," Kathy said.

"And that takes no brains whatsoever," Sylvia said. "Anyway, you need a new fan belt, and you need to have the battery recharged."

"God, Sylvia," Kathy said, "how do you know that?"

Sylvia's father had taught her the most important thing about engines—not to be afraid of them. She'd helped him work on his and had seen that everything had a logic to it. The car's belt pulley had two slots, one was empty, so one belt had broken, and it was the one to the alternator, which recharged the battery, so without it, the battery would run down.

"Never mind," Sylvia said. "It won't be more than about twenty bucks plus tow."

They were in luck. On the other side of the freeway was the Mapledale Mall, and there was a Sears Automotive Center next to it. They crossed the freeway and climbed the fence, not an easy thing to do for Sylvia, the way she was dressed. The man running the service center looked like he was going to throw them out, until Kathy got her father on the phone and had him tell the repairman it was all right to go ahead and fix the car and charge it to his auto-club account. The service manager said it wouldn't take long to put on a new fan belt, but the battery would have to charge up for at least an hour.

"Oh great," Marcie said. "What do we do in the meantime?"

"What *can* we do?" Sylvia said, eyeing the huge mall through the glass doors of the garage. "We go shopping."

The Mapledale Mall was a massive Y-shaped complex, with a central atrium where there were tables and benches, statues, a fountain, a bird cage three stories high, a kidney-shaped goldfish pond, a ring of fast-food franchises for the lower classes on the ground floor, as well as a game room boasting the world's largest collection of video games, and a Cinemas 1-2-3-4-5-6-7-8-9-10. The second floor had a roller-skating rink circling the entire atrium. The third floor was a Babylonian garden of balconies and cantilevered terraces, fancier restaurants for the upper classes, adults who wanted literally to rise above it all, dining amid the ferns and potted palms, while a myriad of reflecting panes of mirrored glass rose overhead like a cathedral, designed to lift the spirits of those below through the skylight and up to heaven. Malls were, in short, Sylvia had always thought, an architect's idea of what paradise would have looked like if God had had enough plastic. She couldn't go to malls without thinking of one of her favorite movies, *Dawn of the Dead,* where three of the last nonzombies on earth take refuge in a mall, and at first they can go into any store they want and try anything on or eat anything or do anything, except that ultimately it becomes so boring and empty that you start to wonder which is the worse hell, being locked up in a prison containing all the material things in the world or being free in a world of zombies. You almost start preferring to be a zombie. Sylvia had begged her father to see it with her, because if anyone were excessively into material things, he was, but to no avail. He liked the movie so much that as soon as they got out of the theater, he bought a VCR so he could rent it and watch it again. Sylvia had been to the Mapledale Mall before, with her mother, but never dressed like a zombie.

"I want to go roller-skating," Marcie said.

"Punks don't roller-skate," Kathy said.

"I forgot," Marcie said, "punks aren't allowed to have fun."

"Not true," Kathy said. "They're just not allowed to actually do anything. You have to just stand around."

Marcie and Kathy laughed, but Sylvia was noticing something. As they entered the mall, a middle-aged man had walked through the door, passing them on his way out, and let the door slam behind him. Not that men had to hold doors open for women, but people shouldn't slam doors in other people's faces, whoever they were. And then the way people looked at her, or maybe more the way they didn't, seeing her and then rudely looking away on purpose, as if to say, *I refuse to acknowledge your existence,* and say it as insistently as the punk style of dress insisted on acknowledgment. It made her feel both conspicuous and invisible at the same time.

"I have to go to the ladies' room," Marcie said. "Or is it the men's room? Androids' room?"

It was easy to make fun of punks in general, Sylvia thought. For all their pretense to originality, they seemed, from one punk to the next, as conformist and unoriginal as any of the other social sets at school— the granolas or the dweebs, dungeon-heads, gear-heads, the chess club. No one much cared, Sylvia surmised, for their sneering cynicism, their attention-calling behavior or for the way punks thought they were cooler than everybody else, even though every-body else thought *they* were cooler than everybody else. In the specific, Sylvia only knew one punk personally, Derek Wideman, and she hadn't really talked to him since seventh grade, and nobody liked him then either, calling him only by his last name because he was overweight. Maybe punks went punk because they felt no one liked them to begin with? And maybe, Sylvia had to admit, people didn't like them because in spite of themselves, they were just slightly in awe of them. At any rate, now complete strangers were sneering at her. Dressing punk wasn't just an antisocial statement—it was a full-fledged antisocial dialogue, a self-fulfilling prophecy.

They passed Pier 1 Imports, a Hickory Farms,

Thom McCann's, Benetton's, a Stride-Rite shoe store, until they stopped in front of Genevieve's, maybe the most expensive store in the mall. There was a beautiful full-length crushed black leather ladies' coat in the window.

"Oh my God, Sylvia," Marcie said. "Black leather is punk, right? Loan me eight hundred dollars."

"It's *you*, Marcie," Sylvia said.

"I *must* have it," Marcie said.

"Well, let's go try it on then," Sylvia said.

"Like this?" Marcie said.

"It's a free country," Sylvia said. "At least it's supposed to be."

They'd barely set foot in the door when the salesperson, a girl only a few years older than they were, approached them, more with the intent to block their way than to wait on them.

"What do you want?" she demanded to know.

"A nuclear freeze?" Sylvia said.

"Pardon me?" the salesclerk said. She was dressed like she'd won her entire wardrobe in a Junior Miss pageant, everything crisply creepy, matching synthetic wash-'n'-toss-in-the-garbage tacky, from the ribbons in her hair down to the webs between her toes. Sylvia took an instant dislike to her.

"We'd like to try on the coat in the window, please?" Sylvia said as politely as possible. The salesgirl snapped her gum in disgust.

"Dream on," she said. "Look, I really don't have time for this, so just go play your stupid little games somewhere else."

"What?" Marcie said.

"Come on, girls," Sylvia said, grabbing her friends

by the arms, "we're buying our ball gowns elsewhere." She led them out of the store. They laughed.

"What a horrible person," Marcie said.

"Look," Sylvia said in a whiny voice, imitating the salesgirl and pushing the end of her nose up with a finger, "'I *really* don't have *time* for this, so just go play your *stupid* little *games* somewhere *else.*'"

"Well gol'," Kathy said, "can you blame her?"

"What are you talking about?" Marcie said.

"I mean, *look* at us," Kathy said.

"You've just been discriminated against," Marcie said. "Wake up and smell the coffee. I think I'll write a book: *Punk like Me.*"

"Kathy, who cares how we look?" Sylvia said. "We're the same people we were before we got dressed tonight, and we deserve the same respect we'd have gotten, dressed normally."

"That was totally awesome," a voice said. The girls turned.

Standing behind them were two punk boys, both in biker boots and zippered, studded black leather jackets. One had a shaved head, over which he wore a tight white bandanna, and the other had a rooster-tail mohawk, dyed blue. The boy with the shaved head introduced himself as Krum, and he said his friend's name was "Drugs, but don't say anything to him because he don't talk. You guys got any smokes?"

"Why doesn't he talk?" Marcie said.

"How should I know? He don't talk," Krum said. "Smokes?"

"We don't . . ."

38

"We ran out," Sylvia said.

"Well, then maybe you got some coin or something?" he said. "We could split a pack."

"We're broke, too," Sylvia said.

"That's a drag, dude," Krum said. Marcie and Kathy were eyeing Sylvia with concern. Sylvia saw no reason for alarm—it was more like a perfect opportunity.

"So what's happening tonight?" she said.

"SOS," Krum said. "Same old stuff. Boring. Everybody's down at the cage." He pointed down the mall. They started ambling in the direction he'd pointed. Marcie tapped Sylvia on the shoulder and mouthed the words, "What are we doing?" to which Sylvia mouthed back, "Just play along." Krum and Drugs both walked with a studied, slouching sort of shuffle. Sylvia tried it, lowering her shoulders and gazing slowly from side to side, but it hurt her knees after a while and she had to stop.

In the atrium, eleven other punks were sitting on the bench encircling the huge bird cage, looking like so many ravens and crows, in proximity to the parrots and tropical songbirds behind the wire mesh. Unless Sylvia missed her guess, there were four girls and seven guys, and enough leather, strapping, zippers, buckles, studs, rivets and assorted hardware to keep the Budweiser Clydesdales in tack for a thousand years. Some had words written on their T-shirts, High Speed Vomit, Death Rhino or Kneel on Me. Others were simply clad in total black. A few nodded or said "Hey" in greeting, while others continued to look around. In fact, for over a minute, nobody did anything except look around, surveying the scene. Kathy seemed impatient, but Marcie was close to giggling. Sylvia leaned over and whispered to Krum.

"What are we looking for?"

"Adventure," he said.

"Oh," she said.

"What's your name?" he asked.

"Yvonne DeCarlo," Sylvia said.

"Where from?"

"The streets," Sylvia said.

"Runaway?"

"Yup."

"Join the crowd," the boy said.

"Where from?" Sylvia asked.

"When?"

"When?" she said. "Now. Where'd you start from?"

"Well, I was born in Omaha," he said.

"God, you're fun to talk to," she said. "Just answer this—is Omaha where your parents are?"

"It's possible," he said. "Who are you anyway—Perry Mason?"

"Excuse me for living," Sylvia said.

"You're excused," he said. "They were in Omaha when I left home, but they moved since then. I think my old man was going to take his girlfriend to Las Vegas to be a showgirl, but she was way too fat to be a showgirl."

"Oh," Sylvia said.

"My mom had cancer, so she's probably dead," he said.

Sylvia tried not to show the shock she felt or give herself away. She figured she'd asked for it. She'd always considered herself a reasonably independent person, even before her parents' separation had forced her to be even more self-reliant than she was naturally. But literally to have no one. No way to get hold of someone in case of an emergency. Not even someone to talk to on the phone about being all alone—it was almost beyond comprehension.

"God," she said.

"Everybody's got problems," he said.

"But," she said, nearly at a loss for words, "if your mother were dying, wouldn't you want to be there?"

"Well," he said, "it would be nice, but for all I know, she'd probably just hang on. I got better things to do than sit around waiting."

Like leaning on bird cages in malls? Sylvia thought. Now she felt almost angry, or at least challenged. How could he possibly mean what he was saying? He was, for certain, not what she'd expected, not a free-lance vegetable with nothing to say and no excuse. He was bright, funny, even nice in his freaky way, and if he was to be believed, he had adequate excuse to be otherwise. He *said* he was bitter, but he seemed awfully casual about it. She wished she could talk to him alone. She had an idea how. She told him she thought she knew where she could scrounge up some cigarettes, if he were still interested. He said he was. Marcie and Kathy didn't want Sylvia to leave them alone, but it looked okay. Sylvia told them she'd be back in ten minutes.

She and Krum walked. Again people stared either intentionally at them or intentionally away from them. One mother picked up her child, the way a mother might at the approach of a mean-looking dog.

41

Sylvia was almost starting to feel like a punk, or like what she imagined Krum must feel, not because she was dressed like a punk, or because she was being treated like one, but because she'd been immediately accepted by a group of them, no questions asked. She looked over her shoulder at all the kids in black, hanging around the bird cage. There were, of course, cliques at school that accepted or rejected you according to how you dressed, but they seemed to be held together, primarily, it seemed to Sylvia, out of a mutual need to impress each other. She'd always assumed the punks, in their own way, by their apparent daring, were much the same. Now it looked more like they hung together because they needed each other—who else would have them? Who else could they count on?

"Penny for your thoughts," Krum said. "Loan me the penny?"

"Nothing," Sylvia said. "What were you thinking?"

"You seem different," Krum said. "That's what I was thinking."

"How?"

"I don't know," Krum said. "Smarter. Not so stuck up, like those others."

"Marcie and Kathy?" Sylvia said.

"Who are Marcie and Kathy?" he said.

"My friends," Sylvia said. She'd forgotten about Pustule and Puke Geyser.

"Oh," Krum said. "I meant the others."

"What's *your* real name?" Sylvia said.

"I really hate the concept of a *real* name," Krum said. "Why should I be forced to admit my relationship to two people who got friendly in the back seat of

a Chrysler Imperial once and made me by *mistake*—
they *told* me—and who hated me and resented me all
my life, instead of just making it easier on all three of
us and having an abortion? You know? I didn't ask for
it, and I didn't have much to say about what my name
was, so I feel I'm free to pick one. The way I figure it,
when I ran away from home, I gave birth to myself, so
I got to name myself."

"Ooooohh," Sylvia said, "that's really beautiful,
dude." She had to snicker. Krum seemed to realize his
answer had been perhaps a little more serious than the
question.

"Okay," he said. "But don't laugh."

"I won't."

"Beryl."

"Beryl?"

"Beryl."

"It's nice to know you, *Krum,*" Sylvia said, shaking
his hand.

"Nice to know you, Yvonne," he said. They were
standing outside a drugstore. Sylvia told the boy to
wait outside, went in and purchased a pack of cigarettes. She wasn't sure what people smoked, but she
thought Marlboros would be safe. He lit one up
immediately, handing the pack back to her. She told
him she was trying to quit. He asked her if she'd
shoplifted the cigarettes. She said did she look like the
kind of person to do that? He laughed.

She asked him about his family. He was reluctant at
first, but then he told her, unemotionally, how his
mother and father, or actually, his stepfather—he'd
never met his father—were both alcoholics, that his
mother used to hit him and his stepfather abused his

sister. She thought of the story David had told her. Krum didn't know where his sister was, either, but he missed her. She'd run away a year before he had—in fact, her leaving gave him the courage. He told Sylvia she sort of reminded him of her. They strolled as they talked.

"I think that was amazingly bold," Sylvia said, "taking off like that."

"You like bold?" he said. "Most people don't know how bold they could be if they had to be."

"Most people don't have to be," Sylvia said.

"So what's your story?" he asked.

"Oh, not much to tell," Sylvia said. "Just your basic tragedy. Papa is a coal miner and Mama works as a waitress in a diner. Poor woman—her biggest dream is to one day get a microwave oven. I just couldn't live there anymore. I'd already decided to take off, and then, about a year ago, Mama told me my papa wasn't my real papa, and she gave me the name of the guy, my real father, who she'd met when he was just passing through town. Said he lived in New York City. I haven't found him yet, but Mama said she thought he might be rich. If he is, I'm gonna get some money from him." Sylvia was hoping Krum didn't watch soap operas, or he'd know she'd just stolen one of the subplots from her favorite, *Ryan's Hope*. "You like television?"

"Chewing gum for the brain," Krum said. "Are you kidding? I love television. Speak of the devil!" They were standing outside a place called Mrs. Dalloway's Gifts, a catalog store full of appliances, dishes, jewelry, knickknacks and, toward the back, a room full of stereos and televisions. "Look, man, my favorite show—*Entertainment Tonight!*" They went in. The manager, a balding fat man in a striped shirt and tie, eyed them suspiciously. *E.T.* was doing a special report on drugs in Hollywood. They watched for a few minutes.

"You know," Krum said, "that's who you remind me of . . . Mary Hart."

"Krum," Sylvia said, "there's not a court in the land that would hold me responsible if I killed you for saying that." He laughed. She looked at her watch. Nearly twenty minutes had passed. "We should be going," she said.

Her back was turned, so she didn't see exactly what happened next. She was leaving the store when she heard Krum shout "Let go of me." She turned to see the fat man, grabbing Krum by the arms, and she saw that the boy had in his grasp a microwave oven. They struggled in the doorway. The store manager was swearing. Krum was trying to break free, and at the same time, he was trying to tell Sylvia, with his eyes, to run for it. She held her ground.

"What's going on?" she said.

"Jimmy!" the fat man called out to his assistant, a thin young man with glasses and a pizza-face complexion. "Grab this creep—he was stealing an oven."

"What?" Sylvia said. The assistant held Krum. The fat man let go of him, came and clamped his fat fist around Sylvia's wrist.

"She was helping him," he said. "Call security. Get his ID." He tried to grab for Sylvia's purse, but she held it away from him. She had to think quick.

"Everybody *wait a minute,*" she shouted. "Let go of him . . . you're scaring him." The store manager paused. "Can't you see he's *retarded?*" she said in a loud whisper. "It's okay, Beryl. We'll be back in the home real soon, I promise. Everything will be okay." Taking his cue, Krum crossed his eyes and let his tongue fall out the corner of his mouth.

"What are you telling me?" the manager said.

"He has *brain damage,*" Sylvia said. "Just look at him—isn't it *obvious?* What's wrong with you anyway?"

"How'd he get brain damaged," the manager asked.

"Spending too much time in malls," Sylvia said. "How should I know? He was born with it. Look, I told him I wanted to buy a microwave, and he just misunderstood me and thought I said I'd already bought it. He loves to carry things. He's harmless—he's just like a puppy, really, aren't you, Beryl?" Krum nodded.

"What does his ID say?" the manager said to his assistant. The assistant took a card from Krum's wallet. Sylvia hoped it wouldn't occur to the manager that it would be unusual for a retarded person to have a driver's license.

"'Tim Breckenridge,'" he read.

Tim Breckenridge? Sylvia thought.

"Call security," the manager said.

"Wait, no," Sylvia said, "we weren't shoplifting, I swear—I want to buy the stupid oven. Look, Amana, my favorite brand. I'm a paying customer."

"Okay, sister," the manager said, "give me $385 or you're going to jail."

Sylvia had no choice but to hand him her American Express card.

"A *gold card?*" the manager said. "*I* can't even get

one of these—how did a creepy little freak like you get a gold card?"

"The same way a sebaceous bozo like you got a store," Sylvia said. "My mother gave it to me." Her mother had, in fact, ordered an extra card for Sylvia, in case of emergencies, and this certainly qualified. "Call it in if you don't believe me."

The manager told his assistant to keep an eye on both of them while he ran a check on the card. When it came up valid, he asked Sylvia for three forms of ID, and when she produced them, he scrutinized them down to the dots over the *i*'s, asking her what her social security number was, and date of birth. When she'd answered all his questions successfully, he had no choice but to begrudgingly write up the charge and sell her the microwave. Sylvia waited until they were out of the store to speak.

"What the hell did you think you were doing?" she said. "Unbelievable! What's wrong with you? You can't just walk out of a store carrying a microwave."

"Bigger things have been stolen," he said. "It was for you."

"What would *I* want with a microwave oven?" she said.

"You said your mother dreamed of having one," he said. "I guess if she wanted one, she could just go out and get one with her *gold card,* couldn't she?"

"Don't call *me* a liar, *Tim Breckenridge,*" Sylvia said. "Where are you from, really?"

"Omaha."

"Where?"

"All over."

"Where?"

47

"Here," he said. "Mapledale."

"Right," Sylvia said, "And your father's a stock-broker, and your mother's a housewife."

"He sells air-conditioning systems," Krum said. "She sells real estate and Amway products."

"Then why did you make up that awful story?" Sylvia said. "And why did you say all those horrible horrible things about them?"

"Because they're so *boring!*" he said. He laughed.

"Now we're getting somewhere," she said.

"They are, they are," he said. "They're boring as hell. They watch the Pro Bowlers tour on television every Saturday afternoon, swear to God."

"That's legal in this country, you know," Sylvia said. They stood at the edge of the atrium. The bird cage was between them and the others.

"I know," he said.

"You didn't have to shoplift," she said. "That's wrong."

"You stole the cigarettes," he said. She stared at him. "You didn't, did you?" She shook her head. "Well, you said you liked boldness."

"Being boldly stupid doesn't impress me," she said. "It's too bad if you can't stand it at home, but it could be worse, you know—my parents split up, my mom's nuts and my dad's so worried about growing old and dull that he just had his ear pierced."

"Don't the other coal miners make fun of him?" Krum said. *"Yvonne?"*

"It's Sylvia," Sylvia said. "We were on our way to a costume party and our car broke down."

"Now we're getting somewhere," he said.

"I'm sorry I lied," she said.

"Me too," he said.

"We don't have room to take everybody," she said, "but I suppose you and your friend . . . uh . . . Drugs, could come to the party if you want. You'd fit right in."

"No thanks," the boy said. "I think I'll just hang out."

"Is that true, what you said about him?" she asked.

"Yeah, it is," he said. "Really. Something bad happened to him, but he won't say what. He listens, he just doesn't answer."

"That's tough," Sylvia said.

"Most of the punks who hang out here have had it tough," he said. "At least they say they have. They could be making it up, too."

"Don't worry about it," Sylvia said. "If that's how they feel, then what's the difference?"

Marcie and Kathy were glad to see Sylvia. They said a cop had come by and told them to move on, but like crows scared from a field by a firecracker, they returned once the noise died down. They wondered why she'd bought a microwave oven. She said she'd explain in the car. They put the oven in the trunk, went to the party and had a great time. When she got home she explained the situation to her mother, and together they returned the oven the next day. The bald fat manager didn't even recognize Sylvia, who was looking her scrubbed, clean and nearly normal self again.

On their way out, they passed Genevieve's. Sylvia asked her mother to wait a moment and went in. The same snotty salesgirl approached her, this time all smiles and obsequious deference.

"Hi," she said warmly, dollar signs flashing in her eyes, "can I help you find anything?"

"Well . . ." Sylvia said, looking the store over, then looking at the salesgirl.

"Anything in particular you're looking for?" the clerk said.

"Actually," Sylvia said, "I saw an outfit like the one you have on, on sale at K mart, but I was hoping for something nicer. I guess I don't see anything here. Thanks anyway."

"What was that all about?" Sylvia's mother asked.

"I just had to pay someone back," Sylvia said.

A Bunch of Kids Were Sitting
Around the Lunchroom

A bunch of kids were sitting around the lunchroom, the day before Thanksgiving break, when Sylvia remembered something she hadn't thought of in years. Everyone was talking about what they were thankful for. Jeremy said he was thankful that there wouldn't be any more school for four days.

"Sure you are," Tommy said. "It's always a rare occasion when you go four whole days without flunking anything."

"Mister Feinman told me he was thankful he wouldn't have to look at your ugly face for four days, too," Adam said.

"I'm also thankful I'm not better friends with you," Jeremy said.

"Me too," Lisa said. All the other girls at the table quickly agreed. Adam blushed in spite of himself.

"Thank you very much," he said.

"I'm thankful for all the tapes Laurie loaned me that I'm never going to return," Ann said.

"Do you think she has any more?" Lisa said.

"Are her parents divorced yet?" Marcie asked. "Do you know, Sylvia?"

"Last week," Sylvia said.

"I'll bet she's thankful for that," Ann said.

I doubt it, Sylvia thought to herself.

"I'd be glad as anything if my parents never said another word to each other for as long as I live," Tommy said.

"I wish they'd never even met," Adam said. Everyone laughed.

"Did I say anything about you?" Tommy said.

"Cry me a river," Adam said.

"What about you, Syl?" Lisa asked. "What are you thankful for?"

It was the combination of thinking about Thanksgiving and the word "river" that triggered the memory, though it had been a lake, not a river. Somehow, in the din of the lunchroom, it was almost easier for Sylvia to daydream than it ever was in the quiet of her bedroom. She remembered reading somewhere that when you dream a dream when you're asleep, hours can pass, inside the dream, but it only takes a few seconds to dream it. The memory was incredibly vivid.

Sylvia was eight or nine years old. It was Thanksgiving. They were all at her grandmother's house in Minneapolis. They'd driven there from Chicago in the old station wagon. She remembered her mother opening the oven door and poking the turkey with a fork. She withdrew the fork. Sylvia was standing beside her. She watched the juices ooze from the four holes the fork made. The smell was as golden as the bird, and it filled the kitchen.

Sylvia's father was in the solarium, watching football. Her cousins Carolyn and Emma were playing in the bedroom with their dolls. Laurel, her one-year-old cousin, was napping. Gramma Grace and Sylvia's Aunt Ellen were in the living room, telling Aunt Ellen's date, Alex, the first man she'd had a serious interest in since her divorce, about Thanksgivings past. Sylvia's mother went and put her arms around her father from behind.

"What's the score?" she asked.

"Fourteen zip, Lions," he said.

"The turkey will be ready at four."

"I need a walk," her father said.

It was a family tradition to take a walk around the lake before the big meal. Both her father's family when he was a boy and her mother's when she was young took walks, to work up appetites. The football game was turned off, still early in the first quarter. The children were assembled and dressed in warm clothing, except for Laurel. Gramma Grace said she'd stay behind to watch Laurel. Alex volunteered to stay and keep Gramma Grace company. In memory, Sylvia thought she knew, even then, that Alex was trying to score points with her grandmother. Her mother was wearing a down vest, Aunt Ellen, a tan windbreaker with a scarf. Her father had on a red sweatshirt. Betsy, the family's golden retriever, was waiting for them on the front steps.

They all walked to Seward Lake, a city lake about two and a half miles across, with a paved footpath-bikepath around it. The leaves had turned, half had fallen, and the air was crisply radiant, rich with autumn. Down the street an old woman was out raking in a camel car parka, her cat watching from the window. There were still pieces of soft pumpkin tossed by Halloween vandals, rotting fragrantly in the road, Sylvia remembered. The children ran ahead. Her cousins used to run with their arms out from their sides, for some reason. At Lakeside Park, they dashed for the swing set. Sylvia's mother called to them to be careful. Sylvia stayed with the grown-ups. A solitary sailboat was buoyed offshore. All the other boats had been taken in. There was one canoe left in the rack.

"Alex is a nice guy," Sylvia's father told Aunt Ellen.

"A hundred times nicer than some of the guys who've asked me out," Aunt Ellen said. Sylvia's mother put her arm around her father's waist. He put his arm around her shoulders. "It's not easy when you have kids."

"So are you going to tell us?" Sylvia's mother said. "Is it serious?"

Aunt Ellen laughed. Sylvia always wanted to be close to her parents, back then, to just stay near them.

"She brought him, didn't she?" Sylvia's father said.

"I remember when she brought Richard for the first time," Sylvia's mother said. Sylvia had always liked her Uncle Richard.

"Richard," her father said.

"Don't laugh, counselor," Aunt Ellen said. "Richard gets the kids for Christmas. He said he's going to introduce them to Bambi then."

"I thought it was Barbara?" Sylvia's father said. Sylvia got the joke.

"She's about Carolyn's age, isn't she?" her mother

said. Part of what Sylvia loved, listening to adult talk, was decoding the things they said in ways they hoped she wouldn't understand.

A stiff breeze blew from the north. The water was high and agitated, but clear. Cold looking. Sylvia's father was saying something about his first and last ice-fishing experience. Emma and Carolyn skipped ahead. Betsy was far in front of everyone, tail wagging, nose to the ground.

"Oh, look," Sylvia's father said suddenly. They stopped. They were halfway around the lake from where they started. In the lee of the wind, a Canada goose squatted resting on the shore, at the water's edge. Sylvia had never seen a goose this close up. The lake was often visited by migrating ducks, but rarely geese, her father said. It stood up, watching them warily.

"He's so big," Sylvia said.

Then a red blur and ferocious growl.

"Betsy—no!" her father said.

The goose saw Betsy coming just in time and managed by wing and foot to leap out into the lake, barely escaping the snapping jaws of the retriever. Betsy was a notorious bird dog, with a history of chasing pigeons. The goose began to swim away from shore, followed by Betsy, paddling as fast as she could, tantalizingly close behind the goose, only a few feet. The goose did not appear to be the least bit worried.

"Betsy!" Sylvia's father called.

"Betsy, you come right back here!" Sylvia said.

"Betsy!" Emma shrieked. Everyone called the dog.

The dog could almost taste the bird, she was so close. It was impossible to call her back. As if to taunt

55

and lure the dog, the goose honked loudly every few seconds and did not paddle any faster than it had to. They were forty feet from shore in no time.

"Betsy, come!" Sylvia's father said with as much authority in his voice as he could muster. He had more control over the dog than anyone in the family. For a second Betsy looked shoreward, but then the goose honked again. "Betsy, heel!" Sylvia's father shouted. The dog ignored him. The goose continued swimming toward the center of the lake, pursued, without possibility, by the single-minded dog.

"Oh my God," Sylvia's mother said. "She's going to die."

"Labs are water dogs, aren't they?" Aunt Ellen said with hope in her voice. The dog and the bird were out of earshot now, pulling away.

"How long can Betsy swim?" Sylvia's mother asked.

"I don't know," Sylvia's father said, "but what difference does it make? The goose can swim forever." No one could believe what they were seeing. "That goose is just going to take Betsy out to the middle and swim in circles until she drowns, just like he would a fox or a coyote. By the time Betsy figures out she's tired, she'll be too far out to make it back."

Sylvia grabbed her mother's leg.

"What are we going to do, Daddy?" Sylvia asked.

"I know I can't swim that well," her father said. "You all wait here. I'll have to find a boat."

"There was a canoe back at the park," Aunt Ellen said.

Sylvia's father set off in the direction they'd come from. He had better than two miles to go. He hadn't started jogging yet and was out of shape. At first, he walked briskly, then broke into a trot.

"Don't have a heart attack," Sylvia heard her mother say under her breath.

In the middle of the lake, the goose was still honking, but Betsy had begun to tire, now fifteen feet behind, still determined.

"Does he know how to canoe?" Aunt Ellen asked.

"A little," Sylvia's mother said. "Once or twice." The children were frightened. Sylvia asked what Daddy was going to do. Her mother told her patiently that everything was going to be all right. He was going to get in the boat and go get Betsy.

The canoe was not locked, only tied by rope. Sylvia's father had difficulty paddling into the wind. He sat in the stern, making the bow rise from the water and catch the wind. The canoe constantly wanted to turn to one side or the other, forcing her father to correct course every two or three strokes. He made slow progress.

Sylvia's mother watched from the shore, helpless. Sylvia hung on to her. All eyes were on the lake. The dog and the goose were hard to spot on the choppy surface, but the honking was audible, though they were over a mile away. Almost there, Sylvia's father missed a stroke, and the wind turned the boat completely around. Sylvia remembered every detail. He reversed, approaching the dog, his red sweatshirt the only color on the lake. The goose veered off. Betsy changed direction. Her father overshot but came around again, putting the canoe between the shore and the dog, so that no one could see clearly what happened next.

Sylvia's father drew up beside Betsy. Paddling into the wind had tired him. He leaned over and grabbed Betsy by the collar. The exhausted dog got her paws on the gunwales, but as Sylvia's father leaned over to pull Betsy in, a strong gust struck the elevated bow of the canoe.

Sylvia saw her father's red sweatshirt disappear. With a horror unlike anything she'd ever known before, she realized her father had fallen out of the boat. Her mother screamed. The canoe didn't capsize, but unoccupied, it was much lighter, rode higher in the wind, and started to blow away. Sylvia's heart was pounding.

"He can't swim," her mother said. She was shaking. Aunt Ellen held her. She turned around to look, but there was no one who could help. Sylvia heard the goose honk. "The water is freezing cold. Oh my God. Oh my God," her mother said. The canoe continued to drift, tossed on the waves. Her father was nowhere to be seen. Aunt Ellen pointed to a house and told Emma to go to it and have someone call an ambulance.

"Oh, Ellen," her mother said. "Ellen. He can't swim. Where is he? I don't see him. Oh my God, I don't see him."

The canoe moved oddly, suddenly, nearly flipping. Sylvia thought she saw something red. And again, red, briefly, but then not again, just the canoe, drifting, blowing toward shore. They ran to where the wind was blowing it. Her mother called out her husband's name, as loud as she could, but there was no reply. Then something moved in the canoe. Betsy's head rose above the gunwales, tongue out, panting. Two hundred yards from shore, Sylvia's father pulled himself up from the bottom of the canoe and managed to wave that he was all right, his arm limp as a noodle.

Her father drifted ashore and jumped out into the knee-deep water. He was soaking wet. Betsy clambered ashore and shook herself. Everyone embraced. Sylvia's mother buried her face in her husband's chest, and he stroked her hair. He grabbed a big handful of it and smelled it. Sylvia saw her father's hand fill with her mother's hair. He said that other than falling overboard and embarrassing himself, his main concern was that he'd lost the paddle and didn't know who to buy a new one for. He was making jokes. Her mother couldn't let go of him. She put her down vest around him when he started shivering. The waves thumped against the canoe. An ambulance arrived, but Sylvia's father told them he was okay. The paramedics looked him over and gave him a blanket. Everyone rode home in the ambulance.

Sylvia remembered sitting in the den, listening to her father explain that maybe it was a good thing he was a few pounds overweight—the extra buoyancy had proven useful. He'd almost thought for a while there, well . . . He'd never been so tired in his life. He spoke calmly. But Sylvia saw that her father and mother had barely been able to take their eyes off each other, from the moment he'd climbed out of the water. And then at the dinner table. The turkey was brought from the kitchen. Gramma Grace was smiling, remembering all the Thanksgivings she'd witnessed before, grateful to see another one. Emma nibbled at her cranberry sauce, picking out the whole berries with her fingers. Carolyn was spreading her napkin on her lap and singing a song about the alphabet. Only Sylvia was old enough to understand what nearly happened, and looked back and forth from her father to her mother. She saw them reach their hands across the table and touch, as if they were rescuing each other from the lake. There was a tear on her mother's cheek.

"What about you, Syl? What are you thankful for?"

"I'm sorry," Sylvia said. "What were you saying?"

"Boy, you're spacey today," Lisa said. "We asked you what you were thankful for?"

"Geese," Sylvia said.

"You have goose?" Jeremy said. "We always have turkey."

"You are a turkey," Tommy said.

Sylvia, to observers in the lunchroom, appeared to space out again, but for a moment longer she wanted to be eight years old and sit at that dining room table one more time. She couldn't believe she'd nearly forgotten that day, the day she almost lost her father. The day she realized he was fallible, not the invincible hero most kids think their fathers are, at first. He could have died. And he was brave. She'd told herself, sitting at the table full of food in her grandmother's house, that if anything ever happened to her like that when she was grown up, it would be her responsibility to look for a boat, too, never be the one watching from shore, because you never know what you're thankful for until you come close to losing it, a lesson, she was eternally thankful, she'd never had to actually learn the hard way.

Sylvia Smith-Smith's
Christmas Surprise

*I*t was the first day back at school after Christmas vacation. Everyone in study hall seemed to be wearing —showing off, whatever—the new outfits they'd gotten as presents. Sylvia Smith-Smith sat with her friends talking. Nobody studied the first day back. Also at her table were The Jennifers. There were three of them, all pretty, all rich—and they'd all been skiing over break, one in Colorado, one in Idaho, and one in Switzerland. They were all back together again, obnoxious as ever.

"So what did you do over break, Sylvia?" Jennifer No. 1 asked.

"I worked," Sylvia said.

"Oh, how awful," No. 3 said. "I'd hate to have to work over vacation."

"I needed the money," Sylvia said. "Working is how a lot of people get money."

"What'd you do?" No. 2 asked.

"Go ahead, tell her," Sylvia's friend Marcie said. Her friends Stephen and Alex nodded.

"I worked as a department-store Santa Claus," Sylvia said.

"Oh, get out of town," Jennifer No. 1 said. *"Really?"*

"We were all there," Alex said.

"No!" No. 2 said. *"Really? That is too cool. How'd you get that job?"*

"It's a long story," Sylvia said. *"Basically I thought I wanted a camera for Christmas, so Marcie and I went into this camera store at the mall, and they had a Help Wanted sign up. We got hired to be Santa's helpers, since the camera store ran the thing so they could charge people to have their kids' pictures taken . . . and then one day Santa Claus suddenly quit, and they had nobody to replace him. I volunteered. It was just supposed to be for one day, but everybody liked me, so I got to keep the job."*

"Great," Jennifer No. 2 said. *"I'd still rather go skiing, though."*

"I think I'd get bored after a few days," No. 3 said. Numbers 1 and 2 concurred. The Jennifers hated it when anyone did anything cooler than they did. They always said they'd probably be bored.

"To tell you the truth," Sylvia said, *"it was probably the most rewarding experience of my life."*

"Why?" Jennifer No. 2 asked.

"Well," Sylvia began . . .

"Ho, ho, ho," Sylvia said in her lowest voice, "and what do *you* want for Christmas?" She sat on Santa's throne high atop North Pole Mountain in the atrium of the Mapledale Mall.

"A doll," a little boy in combat fatigues said.

"Do you want a Barbie doll?" she asked.

"No!" he screamed. He reached up to pull on her beard. She grabbed his wrist and held it. "A G.I. Joe," he said. "I want one that can kill people."

"Oh, now *that's* a good idea," she said. She grabbed him by both arms. "Listen, kid—look in my eyes. If you so much as harm a flea, I swear you'll never see Santa Claus again—do you understand?" The boy nodded, speechless. "Good. Merry Christmas. Next!"

"Ho, ho, ho," Sylvia said. "And what do *you* want for Christmas?"

"A dog," the next girl said.

"What kind of dog?"

"Hot dog."

Sylvia soon learned that you never knew what to expect. The suit was hot, and the beard was itchy. Every tenth kid pulled it. Every eighth kid had a name beginning with the letter *J:* Jason, Jared, Jessica. A third were so nervous they forgot their name. Half the girls under six wanted a My Little Pony doll, the miniature pink or purple plastic horse with the long, shiny, curly mane, a toy so sugary sweet it could give you diabetes. Half the boys under eight wanted The Real Ghostbusters, four-inch vinyl men named Egon and Spengler, and their victims, Mini-Trap and Mini-Shooter. What a racket. She'd never realized, though, what an authority figure Santa Claus was to some children. "Get up there and stop squirming," one mother threatened her child, "or Santa will come and take back the bike you got last year." Sylvia told the child it wasn't so. Children listened to her. Some of these kids really believed it all. It was hard to feel comfortable with that kind of power.

"Ho, ho, ho," Sylvia said. A boy of three sat on her lap, staring up at her in abject terror. She tried jiggling him on her knee. She knew right away she'd made a mistake, but too late—her leg suddenly felt warm . . . and then wet. He'd nailed her good.

"Oh, gross," Jennifer No. 3 said. "That's why I quit baby-sitting."

"Kids can be such brats," No. 2 said.

"Tell me about it," No. 1 said. "I hate skiing with them. You always trip over them. If they can't ski, they shouldn't be on the slopes."

"Tell them about Thurman," Alex said. "Get to the good stuff."

"Why were you guys there?" No. 2 asked.

"To harass us," Sylvia said.

"I didn't mind," Marcie said.

"Actually," Sylvia said, "that was how we met Thurman."

On her second day as Santa, Sylvia noticed Stephen Field and Alex Romine standing beyond the rope barricade, pointing at her and Marcie and laughing. She elbowed Marcie, who was wearing a red elf suit—complete with pointy-toed shoes with bells on them, a long, floppy hat, and Mr. Spock ears. Alex was rumored to have a crush on Marcie. Stephen was the diminutive president of the Young Democrats club at school, a friend whom Sylvia liked to rag.

"Hey, Santa," Stephen shouted. "Don't you think these kids have been corrupted enough by materialism?"

"Keep it to yourself, kid," Sylvia said. "You're just jealous because you're being outdwarfed."

"Hey, Santa," Stephen called out again as he and Alex moved closer to Sylvia's throne, "is that a pillow under your shirt or have we gone off our aerobics regimen?"

"What do you want for Christmas, little boy?" Sylvia said. "Elevator shoes or an oil tanker full of Clearasil?"

"Hi, Marcie," Alex said. Sylvia's first impression of Alex was that he was cute but dumb. Then again, Marcie wasn't the type who sought out challenges.

"Hiii, Alex," Marcie cooed.

"You guys shouldn't talk to Santa Claus like that," someone said. Sylvia looked up in surprise. Her defender was an odd-looking kid, slight, with red hair, a flyaway cowlick, and sleepy gray eyes. He wore white leather high-tops with protruding tongues. They looked big enough to fit him for the next two years. Sylvia had noticed him hanging around earlier but assumed he was waiting for his mother.

"Ho, ho, ho," Sylvia said. "It's okay, little boy. These are friends of mine."

"Yeah, but there are children watching," the little boy said. "Some of these kids are pretty impressionable. They could get the wrong idea." Sylvia had to laugh. He'd obviously overheard his parents talking about impressionable children. It was hard to tell his age—somewhere between an overgrown eight and an undergrown eleven.

"Yes, you're right," Sylvia said.

"We're sorry, kid," Stephen said. "Okay?" The boy seemed satisfied, maybe even a little embarrassed at having spoken up. He blushed and nodded once, then left before Sylvia could find out his name.

"I had the sense he was hiding something," Sylvia told the Jennifers. *"He was really cute and extremely polite, and he sort of had this nervous smile when he spoke."*

"He sounds a little twerpy to me," Jennifer No. 1 said.

"No, I liked him," Sylvia said. *"The weird thing was, he started showing up every day."*

The day after their first encounter she saw him sitting on a bench in front of the Radio Shack. He stayed there over an hour, watching her from a distance. He seemed to be alone. Then she saw him edging nearer, leaning on the velvet-rope barricade, trying to act nonchalant. Whenever she looked his way, he made a little wave. She waved back.

He showed up the next day as well, always wearing the same huge sneakers. The third time she saw him Sylvia decided to take one of her breaks. He smiled as she approached.

"Hello again," she said.

"Hello, sir," the boy said. "I hope you're not angry with me."

"Angry?" Sylvia said. "Why should I be angry with you?"

"Because of what I said to your friends."

"What you said was fine. Santa likes people who speak up for what they believe in," she said. "What's your name?"

"Thurman Westmoreland, Jr.," he said. Sylvia suppressed a laugh. Thurman spoke deliberately, in a raspy, little-man voice.

"Thurman," Sylvia said. "That's an unusual name."

"I was named after the catcher," he said. "He died in a plane crash."

"I know," Sylvia said.

"Can I ask you something?" Thurman said.

"Well, if you want to ask for something for Christmas, I think you should wait in line with the rest of the children," Sylvia said.

"Oh, no," he said, his face lit with alarm. "I know that. I never butt in line, even at school—you can ask anybody."

"Santa knows that, too," Sylvia said. "But what did you want to ask me?"

"Uh, I was sort of wondering if, uh, you needed any more helpers," the boy said. "Sometimes I help my dad in his shop," he added with raised eyebrows.

"Well," Sylvia said, laughing, "Why do you want to be one of Santa's helpers?"

"Because," Thurman said shyly, "I thought maybe I could get one of those employee discounts."

"He told me that was what his mom got where she works," Sylvia said.

"Enterprising kid," Jennifer No. 1 said.

"So what'd you do?" No. 3 asked.

"I gave him a buck and said he could go get me a cup of coffee," Sylvia said.

"Then he started coming almost every day," Marcie

said. "He'd do whatever he thought would be helpful. He got us coffee or sodas; he emptied the photographer's wastebasket; he operated the gate that let kids in. He liked to look important."

"Sounds like a brownnoser to me," No. 2 said.

"But he did have a motive," Stephen said.

"So what was it?" Jennifer No. 1 asked.

"Well, Thurman was trying to play his cards right," Sylvia said, "so he didn't exactly come straight out with it. He waited until two days before Christmas."

Sylvia was in the camera-store office phoning her mom for a ride when she heard a knock on the door. Thurman Westmoreland, Jr., was standing there wearing a brown suit with a poorly knotted red tie.

"Thurman! You look great," Sylvia told him.

"I wanted to make a good impression," he said.

She smiled and waited for him to continue, but he didn't speak.

"Did you want something?" Sylvia said, setting the phone down.

"Sorry to bother you," he said in that little-man voice of his, "but could we have a private talk?" He glanced around the office.

"Sure, Thurman," Sylvia said, still surprised. "I was just calling . . . Mrs. Claus."

"At the North Pole?" the boy asked.

"Yeah," Sylvia said. "She likes me to check in every now and then. What can I do for you?" Sylvia sat behind the manager's desk gesturing to the seat opposite her.

"Well," he said as he sat down, "first of all, just out

of curiosity, what's the most money you've ever spent on one kid?

"Santa doesn't spend money," Sylvia said. "As you know, we make all our own merchandise at the North Pole and then distribute it freely according to who's been bad or good."

"And I've been good, haven't I?" he asked.

"Well," Sylvia said, "it seems you've been very good."

He sighed with relief. "Well, then," he said, trying another approach, "what's the most number of toys you've ever given to any one kid?"

"Well," Sylvia said, "in general, about one each."

"Hmm," Thurman said. He seemed disappointed, but he continued. "What about for special cases?"

"Sure," Sylvia said. "Santa can be flexible. It depends on the situation."

Thurman pulled a piece of paper out of his suit-coat pocket and presented it to her.

Sylvia was amazed. The list was a computer printout of about two dozen items, beginning with a set of walkie-talkies.

"I presume you've prioritized this invoice," she said. He looked puzzled. "You put what you want most first."

"Yeah. The walkie-talkies are what I really want," he said, getting excited but quickly becoming businesslike again. "But everything is equally important. I mean, it would be terrible if any item were left off." He smiled weakly. "Would it be a problem?"

"Well," Sylvia said, astonished at the boy's temerity, "not from a product-delivery standpoint. But

Thurman," she said, leaning toward him, trying not to scold, "don't you think you're being just a little bit greedy?"

He looked alarmed. His eyes darted to the side. "Oh, no," he said. "That's not what they're for. These are for my friends."

"Suure they were," Jennifer No. 1 said.

"That's what I thought, too," Sylvia said. "You should have seen his face—he was absolutely apoplectic. It was totally crucial to him that I bring him everything on the list."

"That's really selfish," Jennifer No. 2 said. "Even I know that."

"Relax—no one's accusing you of anything," Stephen said. Alex smiled and gave Marcie's hand a squeeze under the table.

"It's kind of sad," Jennifer No. 3 said. Number 3 was Sylvia's favorite among the Jennifers, the only one she held out hope for.

"Tell them about the printer," Marcie said.

"Well," Sylvia said, "I looked at the list, and I could tell it had come from a laser printer. Those things are expensive, so then it really puzzled me because if this kid was rich, what was he doing hitting me up for all this stuff?"

The next day she forgot about him in the madness. December twenty-third was the busiest of all. There'd be more last-minute shoppers on the twenty-fourth but fewer children. People were running out of time. Parents were twice as impatient. From Sylvia's high perch the line of hopeful kiddies seemed endless, winding around the atrium birdcage and disappearing behind the Benetton's. She tried to process as many Christmas wishes as she could in the shortest amount of time. She'd looked at so many camera flashes in the past two weeks she was sure she'd have a blue dot permanently branded into each retina.

At ten minutes to closing Sylvia heard a commotion coming from the entrance to Santa's Kingdom. Ordinarily the entrance was roped off at about twenty minutes to nine, and stragglers were told to come back the next day. A security cop was posted there to prevent any arguments. The cop this day was a replacement for the regular one and didn't recognize Thurman Westmoreland, Jr.

"It's okay, Officer," Sylvia said, and Thurman scrambled up the steps.

"I have to tell you something," he said, out of breath. He seemed almost panicked.

"What's up, Thurman?" Marcie asked. "We didn't expect to see you today."

"It's . . . well," Thurman said, "it's something between me and Santa."

"It's okay, little elf," Sylvia said, mouthing to Marcie, *I'll tell you later*. "Calm down, Thurman. What's happened?"

"I just—here." He thrust a small piece of paper toward her. "I forgot when I talked to you yesterday— I'm not going to be at the same address I was last year. Here's the new one. Okay? I'm sorry. I gotta go. Don't forget, okay? It's really, really important." He seemed about to cry. Before Sylvia could stop him, he dropped the paper in her lap and flew down the exit ramp, running toward JC Penney's, bobbing and weaving between shoppers like a fullback.

"What was that all about?" Marcie said.

"We could take your car after work and find out," Sylvia said, looking at the address on the slip of paper.

It had begun to snow heavily, promising the white Christmas everyone had been hoping for. Marcie parked at the curb and bent over to stare up at the building. It was a large mansion on Hinson Boulevard across the street from County Hospital. There was a tall wrought-iron fence around the house, which was also surrounded by a wall of shrubs. The place was dark and foreboding.

"I'd wondered if he was rich," Sylvia said.

"Maybe the kid's a vampire," Marcie said, "and he's always in a hurry because he doesn't want to go monster on us."

"Wait here," Sylvia said.

"No way do I wait here," Marcie said. "It's always the person who waits here who gets it."

They walked up the snow-covered sidewalk. Sylvia didn't know what she was going to say. That she was curious? That Thurman had forgotten something? She decided on the truth: that he seemed inordinately concerned with his Christmas presents and that Sylvia was afraid something might be wrong. She rang the bell. A woman in white pants and a sweater answered the door.

"Yes?" she said.

"Could I speak to Thurman?" Sylvia said. "Thurman Westmoreland, Jr.?"

"Yes, I know," the woman said. "This is regarding?"

"It's kind of complicated," Sylvia said. The woman looked too old to be the mother of an eight-year-old.

"Come in, come in," the woman said. She said her name was Marilyn. The downstairs looked like an ordinary house but different somehow. There were too many couches in the living room. There were no chairs on one side of the dining-room table. There was some kind of escalator going up the staircase, and there was an extremely bright florescent light coming from somewhere toward the back of the house. There was a lit lamp on the end table and next to it a police scanner, screeching with static between broadcasts, with a red blinking light sweeping left to right.

"I'm afraid Thurman isn't here tonight," the woman said. "He'll be back tomorrow. Perhaps I can help you?"

"What is this place?" Marcie said.

"I'm sorry," the woman said apologetically, "this is the Hildreth Foundation. It's a recovery and waiting home for sick children." Sylvia felt stunned. The woman explained. The Hildreths were a wealthy couple who'd lost a child to leukemia and in the child's memory gave the hospital the money to purchase the mansion. Children from out of town who were undergoing chemotherapy were given rooms in the mansion. Often the parents stayed with them as well. Thurman's parents were in Ohio, unable to fly in until the next day. Sometimes children awaiting organ donors also stayed there.

"I know it seems a bit ghoulish," the woman said, "but as you can see," gesturing toward the scanner, "we have to try to stay as ready as possible. Unfortunately the holidays are the most likely time for organ donations because people tend to have more car accidents. If you think of it as life from death, it's not so ghoulish."

"So is Thurman waiting for a kidney or something?" Sylvia said. She wasn't sure she wanted to hear the answer.

"Oh, no," the woman said. "There's nothing wrong with Thurman." Sylvia felt a sigh of relief. "It's his brother Arthur. He needs to have a bone-marrow transplant, and Thurman is the donor. It's a terribly painful process, though."

Sylvia took Thurman's list from her pocket. She explained how Thurman had visited her at the mall.

"We thought he was just going across the street to visit his friends in the hospital," the woman said. "Last night he ran out of here about a quarter past eight and wouldn't tell me where he'd been when he came back."

"He was afraid I wouldn't have the address," Sylvia said.

They pieced together what Thurman had done. He'd used the computer at the hospice to take the Christmas orders for the children too sick to go see Santa, and then he'd done everything in his power to make sure they'd get what they wanted. Sylvia looked closer at the printout. There were two My Little Ponies, a baby carriage, hair ribbons. Now it was obvious. She regretted ever suspecting him of being selfish. She couldn't think of a more selfless act.

* * *

"Sob, sob, what a tearjerker," Jennifer No. 1 said.

"So what'd you do then?" Jennifer No. 3 asked. Sylvia looked at Marcie, who looked at Alex, who looked at Stephen.

"Well," Sylvia said, "it wasn't just me."

"If you ever tell anybody about this, I'll never talk to you again," Stephen said.

"Promises, promises," Sylvia said.

"If the guys on the football team saw this, I'd never hear the end of it," Alex said.

"I think you look real cute in pantyhose," Marcie said. "You've got great legs."

"Better than yours," Stephen said.

"Everybody knock it off," Sylvia said. "This is serious. Act elfish."

It was Christmas Eve and snowing. The twenty-two children occupying the quarters at the Hildreth Foundation were delighted and surprised beyond their wildest dreams when Santa Claus and three elves dropped by to personally deliver the very toys they'd asked for. Parents opened presents for children too weak to do so themselves. Marilyn sat quietly in a room nearby, listening to the cackle of a police scanner. Santa Claus kissed the heads of the kids whose hair had fallen out from chemotherapy. A big tall elf danced with one child by spinning him around in his wheelchair, and a skinny little girl with a plastic ID bracelet played the piano. Thurman stood away from the crowd. His parents sat on the couch with his brother Arthur. Thurman and Santa Claus, standing on opposite sides of the room, exchanged knowing glances and smiles.

"Where'd you get all those toys from?" Jennifer No. 2 asked. "Did some store donate them or something?"

"No," Sylvia said. "We bought them."

"Sylvia bought them," Stephen said.

"Where'd you get the money?" Jennifer No. 3 said.

"I told you already—I worked for it," Sylvia said. The bell signaling the end of study hall rang. Jennifers 1 and 2 appeared to be extremely uncomfortable now in their expensive new outfits and their skiing tans. One couldn't look Sylvia in the eye.

"All those toys are probably broken already," the other said.

"Oh, I hope so," Sylvia said. "I hope they played with them so hard they broke into a million pieces."

Jennifer No. 3 waited until she had a chance to speak to Sylvia alone. Her mascara had run slightly at the corner of her eyes. She spoke so that no one else would hear.

"Sylvia?" she said. "Look, I know you don't particularly like me or my friends, okay? Maybe they, or we . . . can't help being the way we are, or maybe we can; I don't care. But I just wanted you to know that I think what you did was a really great thing."

"Well, it wasn't really me; Thurman's the hero here," Sylvia said.

"How is he?" Jennifer asked.

"They're both fine," Sylvia said. "They went home yesterday."

"Great," Jennifer said.

* * *

Sylvia hadn't told anybody, however, about the phone call she'd received on Christmas Day. A familiar voice asked to speak to Miss Sylvia Smith-Smith.

"Speaking," Sylvia said.

"Hello, Miss Smith," the voice said, "this is Thurman Westmoreland, Jr., calling."

"Yes?" Sylvia said. "Do we know each other?"

"Aw, come on," the boy said. "I wanted to thank you for last night in person because I thought that was really nice."

"What was?" Sylvia said. There was a pause.

"Aren't you the person who worked as Santa Claus at the Mapledale Mall?" he asked. "That's what they told me. This is Thurman—Thurman Westmoreland, Jr."

"I don't know what you're talking about," Sylvia said. "I was at a party with my friends last night, and then I came straight home."

"Are you telling me the truth?" he asked.

"Absolutely," Sylvia said. "You can talk to my parents if you don't believe me." There was a long silence.

"Well, then who delivered the presents last night?" the boy asked.

"I don't know," Sylvia said. "What did he look like?"

Another pause. "I'm going to have to give this some consideration," the boy said. "Thank you, though. Sorry to bother you."

"Anytime," Sylvia said.

Sylvia and the Visitor

Sylvia Smith-Smith sat on the living room couch, with everything she could possibly want at her fingertips. The telephone was to her left, the remote control to the color television was on her lap, under a paperback book entitled *Laidmoor's Lady,* and on the end table, to her right, there was a bowl of nachos, a liter of diet soda and a glass of ice. Spread out on the coffee table before her was a game of Trivial Pursuit, which she liked to play solitaire. Kids at school were playing it in Study Hall, and Sylvia was undefeated. Everyone wanted her on his team. It was probably the only actually educational thing anybody had ever done in Study Hall since the beginning of time, so of course the principal was trying to have it banned. Someday, Sylvia thought, I'll understand old people. That will be a sad day. Why did they want to control everything all the time?

No one was controlling her now. There were no adults in the vicinity. She was at her mother's, but her parents were both gone, mother visiting her sister Ellen in California, father in Texas on business. She had the whole house. It was becoming spring. Sylvia was alone, gloriously, peacefully alone. Except, of course, for Betsy.

"Hey, Betsy," Sylvia said. "I need your advice. Do I finish this stupid romance novel, do I watch Richard Gere in *Breathless* on cable for the fifteenth time, or do you want to play another round of Pursuit?"

Betsy looked at her as if to say, "Whatever you want, you slob."

"Good idea," Sylvia said, "Richard Gere it is." She took the remote control and turned on the TV. "You know what else? We're going to order a pizza." Sylvia still had plenty of money, from what her mother had left her. "What do you want on it? Sausage? Pepperoni?" Neither suggestion got much of a response from Betsy. "Sausage," Sylvia decided.

Betsy was lying on the floor at Sylvia's feet, head propped up on a pillow, glancing at the television from time to time, but mostly sleeping. Betsy wasn't much into Richard Gere. At fourteen, Betsy was three years younger than Sylvia. Sylvia couldn't remember a day in her life when she hadn't spent time with Betsy. They'd played together, in every room of the old house, all over the lawn, all around the old neighborhood, before Sylvia's parents separated. They'd walked to school together every day. Betsy used to wait for Sylvia at the door to walk her home, too. They'd taken all their vacations together. Once, Sylvia refused to go to summer camp when Betsy couldn't come along. When Sylvia had no one else to talk to, feeling like an only child, she'd always had

Betsy. Because Betsy was an only dog, a golden retriever, a little deaf, a little overweight and a whole lot lazy.

"Hey, old lady," Sylvia said, when the pizza came, "I hope you know that all this luxury stops when Mom gets home. Then it's back to dog food. For both of us." She ate half the pizza, then set the other half on the floor in front of Betsy's nose. No one had ever wondered how Betsy got to be overweight. Sylvia fell asleep on the couch, before she even had a chance to see Richard Gere with his shirt off. She awoke, some time in the middle of the night, and practically without opening her eyes, turned off the lights and stumbled away to bed. When she got up the next morning, she took a shower, got dressed and went to the kitchen. She ate breakfast, went into the living room, and noticed that Betsy had not touched the pizza. It was only then that she knew something was seriously wrong with her dog.

Sylvia Smith-Smith had never quit at anything, never, for example, stopped hoping—hoping wasn't even the word—never stopped knowing for sure that one day her parents would get back together, that every part of her life would work out. It had to—those were the rules. "Perseverance, dearie," her mother always said. "Hard work," her father counseled, his life's motto. Sylvia wasn't worried. She called the veterinarian, told him Betsy had lost her appetite and then took the old girl in, in a taxicab. Betsy jerked feebly in Sylvia's arms at the smell of the vet's office—she hated the vet's—but was too sick to put up much of a fight. The vet was a middle-aged, kindly, balding man named Dr. Elgin. He laid Betsy on her side on the stainless steel examining table. He looked in her eyes, her ears, then probed Betsy's side with his fingers. He asked Sylvia how long Betsy hadn't been eating.

"Well," Sylvia said, "I guess she hasn't touched her bowl for a couple of days, but I didn't worry about it because she's so fat. When old Bets turns down pizza, though, you know she's got a stomachache. She once ate an entire large with anchovies and mushrooms that we left sitting on the table. It was our fault. Anyway, it was pretty funny."

"Uh-huh," the doctor said, still feeling the dog's side. "Put your hands here, Sylvia, I want you to feel something." Sylvia obliged. "Do you feel those lumps? Kind of like little hard-boiled eggs, under the skin?"

"Yeah?" Sylvia said.

"I'm afraid Betsy has more than a stomachache," the doctor said. And then suddenly Sylvia saw the awfulness, a kind of terrible horror, like shadows filling in the corners of the room, and she knew what the doctor was going to say before he said it. "Betsy has cancer, Sylvia. It's quite metastasized." Sylvia had nothing to say, she was too shocked. "I think it would be best if we called your parents and had them come in." But Sylvia willed herself to concentrate, and then all she could feel was the heart beating inside of Betsy, the way it always had, not the lumps, not the disease at all.

"No," Sylvia said.

"I'm sure you know, Sylvia," the doctor said, "that if Betsy were a human being, she'd be in her nineties.

You're really quite fortunate that she's lived this long. We all wear out, and it's not bad. It's perfectly natural."

"No."

"Sylvia," Dr. Elgin said, "can't you see that all Betsy wants is to go to sleep and rest? We can see when dogs want this, and we have things to help them."

"No-no-no-no-no!" Sylvia said. The doctor waited for her to calm down. "Is she in pain?" Sylvia asked, finally.

"I think not," the doctor said. "When it's merciful, the disease somehow separates the pain center in the brain from the body, and the dog doesn't feel much pain. Maybe just a little. Even so, Betsy is going to die, Sylvia."

"When?" Sylvia asked.

"In a week, maybe," he said. "It could be much sooner. We should call your folks."

"We can't," Sylvia said. "They can't be reached. They're away."

"Sylvia," Dr. Elgin said, "in that case, I think it would be best if we—"

"Look, I know, okay?" she said. "I know. Just not now, okay? Just not now. I'll think of something."

"Sylvia . . ."

She'd always thought of something. She'd never known what that something was going to be, before the moment she thought of it, but she'd always managed to come up with a plan.

It was difficult at first for Sylvia to hold Betsy, feeling, then, the lumps, the proof she was trying to deny. Yet holding and petting her were all the ways

Sylvia could imagine to comfort her. They sat together on the couch. Betsy was clear-eyed, but tired. Sylvia had made Betsy a dinner of her favorite foods, liver, cheese and ice cream, but Betsy barely sniffed at it. Sylvia talked to Betsy, nonstop.

"Remember when you stole my favorite doll?" Sylvia would say. "I loved Mrs. Mcgillicuddy, and you knew it, but what was I going to do—my stupid dog is walking around the house with my doll in her mouth, and every time I tried to get it away from you, you ran behind the couch. You dumb mutt. I'll bet you don't even remember. And then the vet said, not Dr. Elgin but the other one from the old house, that female dogs get motherly instincts, and sometimes they pick up a doll or a shoe or a stuffed animal, and carry it around like it was a puppy. And then Dad said we should have you spayed. I said . . ."

Sometimes Sylvia felt self-conscious, talking to the dog. Sometimes she wondered if she were cracking up. Sometimes she'd look down, though, and have to stop to cry. She'd never felt so hopeless, or so alone. There was no one she could call, and nothing anybody could do, even if she could get a hold of them. So she lay on the couch, holding on to Betsy, trying to think of something. The TV was on low, but everything on it seemed ridiculous, stupid and trivial, she thought. She fell asleep somewhere in the middle of Johnny Carson.

Sometime after midnight there was a knock at the door. Sylvia got up and answered it. It was a man, about thirty, nice looking, shy, and for some reason, Sylvia felt she could trust him, so she let him in.

"Hi," he said. "I'm here to take Betsy."

"Are you from the vet's?" she asked.

"No, I'm afraid not," he said. And then Sylvia knew where he was from and who he was.

"You're Death, aren't you?" she said.

"Not exactly," he said. "You can call me that if you want, but there's no one guy named Death. It's more like a car pool. We all work in the same department. I just do pickups—the higher-ups make all the decisions. Nice house."

"Thanks," Sylvia said.

"Is this Betsy?" he said, moving over near the couch.

"That's her," Sylvia said.

"She's beautiful," he said.

"You should have seen her when she was younger," Sylvia said.

"I can imagine," he said.

"Are you hungry?" Sylvia asked. It seemed like a perfectly logical thing to ask, though everything else about the visitor felt illogical and strange.

"A little," he said. "What have you got?"

"I could warm some pizza in the microwave."

"Pepperoni?"

"Sausage," she said.

"Brother. I haven't had pizza since I don't remember when. Just a little, if it's no trouble, and then I really should be going."

Sylvia went into the kitchen. The beginning of a plan was forming in her head. It seemed odd that she'd been able to delay Death on his mission. Maybe she could thwart him altogether, if she could think of a way. When she came back to the living room with the warmed-over pizza, Death was sitting on the couch, patting Betsy and studying the coffee table.

"What's this?" he asked. Sylvia hadn't cleaned the room from the night before. To be honest, she hadn't cleaned a thing since her parents left.

"Trivial Pursuit," Sylvia said. "It's a game. Here, I'll show you." She pulled out a card from the deck of questions and read him one, the easiest one she could find. "Who wrote 'Roll Over Beethoven'?"

"Chuck Berry," Death said.

"See?" Sylvia said. "Some are easy, some are hard. You roll the dice, and then you get to pick from different subject areas, whatever you land on, and then you move these round things around, filling them in with different colored wedges whenever you can answer a question correctly, until you get them all, and then the first person in the middle wins. It's really fun."

"It looks like it," Death said. "This is great pizza."

"You shouldn't talk with your mouth full, you know," she said. She could feel herself gaining in confidence. "You want to play a game, maybe, or are you in a hurry to get somewhere?"

"No hurry," Death said, "It's a slow night. We're not really supposed to play games. I used to be pretty good at chess."

"This is more fun than chess," she said. "One game. Then afterward, you can take Betsy."

Death had to think about it.

"Okay," he said.

"If you win," Sylvia said. "But if I win, Betsy can stay one more year."

"Sylvia."

"How ungrateful do you get?" she said. "I invite you in, you make yourself at home, you eat my pizza and then you want to steal my dog like you have no manners whatsoever."

"Okay," Death said, throwing up his hands. "All right." He rubbed his palms together in anticipation, looking at the game spread out on the coffee table. "It looks like I'm going to have to teach you a lesson."

"You're all talk," Sylvia said jokingly. She could hardly contain the joy she felt. It was a reprieve, a second chance, and not even her parents were as good at Trivial Pursuit as she was—she was a natural-born whiz—everybody said so.

Death chose blue, and Sylvia chose green. They rolled the dice, and Sylvia had a six, so she began. She went straight for her specialty, art and literature. The question was, "What Ray Bradbury novel is named for the temperature at which paper catches fire?" Not only was she a whiz, but luck was on her side—she'd just finished reading that very book, not two weeks before.

"Fahrenheit 451," she said. One move, and she already had her first piece of the pie.

Nevertheless, Death was a formidable opponent. He was weak on sports and entertainment, but very good at geography, since he'd been everywhere, and science, and virtually unbeatable in history, since he'd met most of the people in the questions who'd died, long before Sylvia was even born. One question asked the name of the Las Vegas hotel that burned in 1980, taking eighty-four lives, and Death could name not only the hotel, but all of the victims. He was so-so in art and literature, since his job didn't give him much time to read. Sylvia could have creamed him, she knew, at the Baby Boomer edition, which had a lot of rock and roll questions, but unfortunately, they were playing the Genus edition. For two hours she held her own, coming up with answers that surprised even her, like "What year did Hitler become chancellor of Germany?—1933." As they played, one would have the advantage, then the other, in a see-saw battle. By the time they reached the final question, they were even. Sylvia was calm, even though so much depended on the outcome. She rolled the dice and picked art and literature.

"What materials," Death read from the card, "did the Three Little Pigs use to build their houses?"

"You lose, Big D," Sylvia said. "I knew that one when I was two years old. Straw, sticks and stones."

"Bricks!" Death said, throwing the card down. "Not stones, bricks—fooled you, fooled you." He laughed wickedly. Sylvia couldn't believe she'd missed that.

"It's the same thing," she protested.

"Oh, of course it isn't," Death said. "My turn. Gimme the dice. Gimme gimme gimme."

"Don't be so greedy," Sylvia said. He rolled, and picked history.

"Who," Sylvia read, "was Barry Goldwater's 1964 vice-presidential running mate?"

"Oh my goodness," Death said. "Who in the world could remember that?"

"You mean you can't?" Sylvia said.

"No," Death said.

"William Miller," Sylvia said. "You should know that. He was the first guy to do those American Express commercials."

"I don't watch TV," Death said. "Too much violence. I like game shows, though."

Sylvia had one more chance. She took a deep breath and sipped the last of the diet soda she'd poured herself, back when the game began. She rolled, and opted for entertainment. The question was, "Who recorded the 1959 hit single 'Mack the Knife'?" It just happened to be her father's favorite song, the one he'd sung to her when she was little.

"Bobby Darin!" she shouted out. "I win." An incredible sense of relief washed over her. Death seemed to be taking the loss magnanimously. "Thank you so much, Mr. Reaper, but now if you don't mind, please get out of my house and don't come back."

"You're welcome," the man said. He stood up, looked at Sylvia, then at Betsy. He whistled softly, and said, "Come on, Betsy, time to go." Betsy suddenly opened her eyes and jumped down from the couch.

"What?" Sylvia said, as furious as she'd ever felt. "No fair! No fair at all. I beat you fair and square. You said she could stay one more year." Sylvia was sobbing.

"No," Death said, "I said I was going to teach you a lesson. I think you're starting to get it now. You're right; it isn't fair. It never will be fair, but if you look hard enough, you'll see that it's right. You can't always win, Sylvia. You have to accept that this is right."

"No," she said.

"Yes," he said. "Look." Betsy was standing by the door, wagging her tail, waiting to leave, obviously both ready and willing. Sylvia accepted that much.

"Where are you taking her?" she had to ask.

"It's really quite difficult to explain," the man said. "The part you know, the physical part, of course, dissolves. The part you don't know, except that it's what made Betsy Betsy, goes back to where it came from before it was Betsy. It has to go back, Sylvia. It can't stay forever."

"Why not?" she said.

"It just can't," he said.

"So it doesn't matter then," Sylvia said. "I mean, you can love something and take care of it, and it just doesn't matter in the end, does it? You're just going to come take it away."

"Sure it matters," the man said. "Remember six years ago at the beach, when Betsy almost got hit by a car, and you called her back? If you hadn't trained her to mind you, she would have died then. Her name was on the list, but it turned out it wasn't right. Not that day."

"Really?" Sylvia said.

"Really," the man said. "Loving her gave her six more years. It makes all the difference in the world."

The man walked to the door. In the meantime, Betsy had found the bowl of liver, cheese and melted ice cream, and was wolfing it down.

"Betsy," the man said firmly.

"You have to call her at least three times," Sylvia said.

"Betsy," he said again. The old dog took one last

gulp, then turned and went to Sylvia. Sylvia got down on her knees and hugged Betsy as hard as she could, ran her hands along her sides. The lumps were gone. Betsy licked Sylvia's face.

"Go with him," Sylvia said, "good girl."

Betsy followed him to the door.

Of course it was only a dream, but when Sylvia awoke, Betsy was dead. Sylvia wrapped the part of Betsy she knew in a blanket and took it down to the vet for disposal. Walking home by the park, Sylvia could easily imagine the part of Betsy that only Betsy had known, off being a regular dog somewhere, in some different, unknowable way.

She spent the two days she had until her mother came home cleaning the house during the day and reading at night. When she couldn't read, she'd put her book down and think about Betsy. There were no bad memories, only good ones. Betsy jumping on her bed in the morning; Betsy sitting still for fourteen Christmases, while the family hung around her neck the ribbons from unwrapped packages and then took her picture; Betsy sleeping in a sunbeam, with her paws moving in a running dream. And she thought about the dream she had, what it might have meant. She was Sylvia Smith-Smith, clever and resourceful, but the dream seemed to tell her that for the first time she could remember, she'd failed, but that failure wasn't bad. She was pretty sure the visitor was some figment of her imagination she'd created, half Dr. Elgin and half Richard Gere. Her favorite part of the dream was when she learned that loving things, even

"Oh no," her father said. "I guess I blew that one."

"It's okay, Daddy," Sylvia said.

"Maybe we can trade it in on some peripherals," he said. "You know, accessories, to . . . ah . . . enhance what your mother bought you."

He took her shopping the next day. The salesman said there was no problem, swapping hardware for software. The programs were "user friendly," but Sylvia found herself "computer hostile." Her father wanted to buy her a financial-management program, but she doubted she needed one, on an allowance of five dollars a week. She let him have his way.

"How about data-base management? You can keep track of all your baseball cards."

She wondered what was wrong with the cigar box she'd been using.

"We'll need a modem," her father told the salesman. "These things are great. You hook them to the telephone, and then—"

"Thanks, Daddy."

"And then of course, a game library would—"

"Thanks, Daddy."

So let the world be destroyed, she thought, sitting in her room. Over and over again. Foreign invaders.

"Sylvia," the lawyer had said, "I hope you understand that in all likelihood, you won't have to testify, and if you don't want to, nobody's going to force you, but the judge might want to invite you back to his office to ask you a few questions, what it's been like at home and so on. It's really not unpleasant. Lots of kids have done it."

Thanks to guys like you, she wanted to say. What she would have given to get him in a video game and drop a few photon torpedoes in his briefcase. Maybe it wouldn't let her have birthdays with both her parents at the same time again, but it would sure make her feel better.

She picked up her bedroom telephone and dialed her father's office, but her finger hit the wrong button on the last digit, a nine instead of a six. No answer. Instead, only a high-pitched tone. She hung up to dial again, then realized she'd dialed her father's company computer by mistake. Only other computers made that particular tone. She'd been playing with her own modem for a month and had figured out how they worked. She turned hers on, dialed the number ending in nine again and put the phone in the modem. Her screen lit up.

HELLO. USER IDENTIFICATION, PLEASE.

DAVID SMITH-SMITH, she typed. A name he'd never liked.

NO NAME IN FILE.

DAVID ALAN SMITH, she typed. Her father's real name.

HELLO. Her father didn't like the hyphenated version, either.

PROGRAM MENU, PLEASE.

Sylvia really had no idea, at first, exactly what she was looking for. It was like rummaging in her parents' drawers. She'd done it a few times, back when they lived together. All kids did it, she thought. The data base would be the drawer with the most junk in it. A lot of it had to do with stockbrokering, client investment records, econometric reports and so on, but one file caught her eye: PERSONNEL.

The computer asked her how she wanted to sort it. Sylvia, this time, knew exactly what she was looking for. Her mother had told her, preparing her for the hearing, something she said was sure to come out, so she might as well know.

WOMEN HAVING AFFAIRS WITH MY FATHER.

INCORRECT INSTRUCTIONS. PLEASE CHECK HELP MENU.

WOMEN, FROM YOUNGEST TO OLDEST.

PLEASE WAIT.

Sylvia's mother had said it was someone at work. The word she'd used to describe the girl was "cupcake."

GWENDOLYN S. MILLER
BORN 3/14/60
519 WEST END APT 24
555-8152
BA MT HOLYOKE 1980
DATA PROCESSING 8/4/82--PRESENT

Probably not the one, Sylvia thought. Too recently hired. Sylvia's mother said the affair began when she and Sylvia were in Europe, the summer of 1982. Sylvia wondered why she'd never suspected.

JAN T. CALDEWELL
BORN 6/9/59
351 E. 82ND #4D
555-8475
MA ENG COLUMBIA 1980
MBA COLUMBIA 1982
DATA PROCESSING 3/14/81-- 4/22/82

DATA PROCESSING MGMT 4/23/82--10/25/86
JUNIOR BROKER 4/26/86--PRESENT

Promoted to data processing management in April of the year her father started fooling around. This looked suspicious. Sylvia called up Jan Caldewell's file. Raised in East Hampton, probably wealthy, cultured, pretty, things that would appeal to her father. The tip-off came at the end of the file, something her father had forgotten to delete:

WHAT TO BUY TO CELEBRATE PROMOTION:
DOZEN ROSES
BLACK DRESS--SAKS
TEDDY BEAR

Sylvia couldn't believe her father had bought his girlfriend a teddy bear. The magic of computers, she knew, was that you could change anything in them. She added to the list.

BRACES
TRAINING BRA

She laughed. It would all come out at the hearing tomorrow anyway. The aliens invading her life would have their way.

"Syl," her mother had warned her, "remember darling, it's just a game, really. They say things, we say things, and both sides exaggerate to make their cases look better. That's what my lawyer told me, sweetie. Your father and I will still be friends, whatever happens."

Aliens. Gray old men lighting cigars and deciding her fate in back rooms. For the last six months there was never anything she could do about it, beyond helping her mother out and carrying messages back and forth between two people who had once loved each other so much: Sylvia had been helpless.

Until now. She'd never had her own computer before.

She called up her father's correspondence file, form letters, where all you had to do was type in the name of the person you wanted to send a letter to, and the computer did the rest. She scrolled through the form letter until she found what she was looking for.

INTEROFFICE

DEAR _____

   WE REGRET TO INFORM YOU THAT YOUR SER-VICES WITH THE COMPANY NO LONGER MEET OUR EMPLOYMENT NEEDS. WE ARE GRATEFUL FOR SERVICES RENDERED SO FAR, BUT HAVE DECIDED . . .

Sylvia typed in Jan Caldewell's name, instructed the computer to transmit immediately, pushed the button, and it was done. No doubt they'd figure it out, but at least it would shake things up. Let Jan Caldewell cry into her teddy bear for a night. How many nights had Sylvia cried?

Sylvia had another idea of whom she wanted to send a letter to.

DATA BASE PLEASE.

NAME OF FILE?

LEGAL.

She found the name of her father's lawyer and called the number listed there. A secretary answered. Sylvia hung up. She called the number again, seven times, changing the last digit each time until she got the computer tone. She put the phone back in the modem.

DENHAM, MYERS, WOERNER AND ASSOC., AT-TORNEYS AT LAW

USER IDENTIFICATION?

What was her father's lawyer's name?

RUSSELL MYERS

NO NAME IN FILE.

RUSSELL B. MYERS

NO NAME IN FILE.

RUSSELL C. MYERS

NO NAME IN FILE . . .

She went through the alphabet. His middle initial was *S*. *S* for shyster.

HELLO.

Sylvia was amazed. Hadn't these people heard of passwords?

She called up the program menu, asked for the data base, specified for DIVORCE and eventually got her father's case on the screen. She read the information there with interest, what her father's income was, her mother's, what their joint property amounted to. She couldn't believe the house she'd grown up in was worth one hundred fifty thousand dollars, but again, she knew these things would be overestimated. Part of the "game."

All she planned to do was fire her father's lawyer, but she scrolled ahead, just to see what was there. She came to a document called Interrogatory, a list of names, places, dates and questions about the marriage, which her father had answered. Sylvia had been sent to her room the night her mother had had to fill hers out.

QUESTION 3
FOR EACH PERSON, MALE OR FEMALE, WHO HAS RESIDED WITH YOU, OR WHO HAS SHARED A ROOM WITH YOU FOR ANY PERIOD OF TIME LONGER THAN ONE DAY DURING THE MARRIAGE, OR WHO HAS TRAVELED WITH YOU, PLEASE STATE: NAME, ADDRESS, EMPLOYER, DATE AND PLACE OF EACH EVENT.

Her father admitted to traveling with Jan Caldewell, 351 E. 82nd #4D, to a three-day meeting in Boston, the summer of 1983. It said they stayed in the Sheraton, in separate rooms.

QUESTION 6
STATE WITH REASONABLE PARTICULARITY ALL THE FACTS THAT SHOW ALLEGED FAULT OR MISCONDUCT ON THE PART OF THE PARTY . . .

Sylvia couldn't believe her eyes. Her father claimed her mother abused drugs, had been addicted to Valium since 1980. Sylvia remembered finding a box of little yellow pills once. Once.

"Birth control, darling," her mother had said, "you know all about that, don't you?"

Sylvia didn't, so she kept sneaking into her parents' room and counting the pills. She wanted to know how many she took. The bottle had lasted over a year. Why did her father use the word *addicted*? Furthermore, her father claimed her mother had a drinking problem. This was absurd. Sylvia had seen her mother drunk twice in her life, and the last time her father had been loaded, too—they came home from a party, put *Swan Lake* on the stereo and hopped around the room laughing, pretending they were ballet dancers. Why was her father lying? If this was part of the divorce game, it wasn't funny anymore, not when it meant saying hurtful untruths about the other person, just to make your case look better. He went on to say her mother neglected Sylvia, leaving her home alone to fend for herself. Well, of course! She was old enough to fend for herself.

QUESTION 8
STATE WITH REASONABLE PARTICULARITY DIF-
FERENCES YOU CONSIDER IRRECONCILABLE,
WHEN EACH DIFFERENCE AROSE, AND THE
EFFORTS YOU'VE MADE TO RECONCILE EACH
DESCRIBED DIFFERENCE, WITH REFERENCE
THERETO, INCLUDING . . .

For three months, in the fall of 1982, back when it was starting, according to her parents' answers, they'd gone to see a marriage counselor, every Tuesday night. They'd told Sylvia they'd joined a bridge club.

Sylvia read with tears in her eyes. After her father's interrogatory was over, her mother's appeared. Apparently, the lawyers had exchanged copies, playing games, preparing their little tricks. Her mother's document described the affair her father was supposed to have had. It said he also abused alcohol, had an uncontrollable temper and had even hit Sylvia on several occasions. Sylvia could remember only one occasion, the time she'd gotten caught shoplifting a bracelet, when she was nine. She'd gone wrong, she knew, she'd said so at the time, and it had only been a spanking. It didn't even hurt—she was too old to spank, but her father didn't know what else to do, and he said he was sorry afterward.

They were both lying. Sylvia could understand why you might have to exaggerate in order to get something, but the point was, none of it mattered. The point was, they were both lying. Sylvia believed in the truth. If some judge was going to read this, he should at least know the facts. There was nothing for her to do but erase what her parents had written and start over, first her father's, then her mother's. The truth, according to Sylvia.

When she was done, she made a safety copy of her work on a floppy, dialed into her mother's lawyer's computer (they didn't know about passwords, either) and made sure both versions read the same. She'd just finished when her mother knocked on her bedroom door.

"Supper's ready," her mother said. "What are you doing, love?"

"Playing games," Sylvia said.

* * *

The judge was a small man with thinning hair and half glasses that sat on the end of his nose, making him look like one of the Seven Dwarfs. He seemed like a fair man. Sylvia's mother wore a blue business suit. She'd wanted Sylvia to wear a dress, but Sylvia refused, compromising at a nice pair of pants and a sweater. Her father sat across the aisle in gray pinstripes, with his lawyer, who had tried to get Sylvia to sit with them.

Smith-Smith v. *Smith-Smith* was the second case on the agenda. The first was that of a young couple who agreed they'd married too young, parting amiably with a brief sad kiss. Then the bailiff called for Sylvia's parents. The lawyers moved forward. The judge asked if an agreement had been reached.

"We have not, Your Honor," Russell Myers said. "Your Honor, if it please the court, we'd like to ask for a continuance at this time."

"On what grounds?" the judge said.

"We were unable to locate a witness this morning, Your Honor," Russell Myers said. "A Ms. Jan Caldewell." "Was she subpoenaed?" the judge asked.

"No, Your Honor, but we believe her testimony would be crucial to our argument, and we ask . . ."

"Your Honor," Sylvia's mother's lawyer, a man named Fahey, said. "We also so move, on the same grounds."

"Where is she?" the judge asked, peering over his glasses.

"We don't know, Your Honor," Russell Myers said.

Sylvia was tempted to snicker.

"I'm going to deny here," the judge said. "Let's see

what we can do without her. You've both had four months, and we've already rescheduled once, and to be frank, I don't have time to wait for counsel who can't secure their witnesses. You have the interrogatories?"

Both lawyers, looking like punished dogs, took papers from their briefcases and presented them to the judge. Not the copies they'd read over, with the notes they'd made in the margins—fresh clean copies, hot off the computer.

The judge began to read. At first he looked angry to Sylvia, but then he smiled a few times, and actually chuckled once. When he was done, he took his glasses off and wiped them on his robe, looking straight at Sylvia. He put his glasses back on.

"With counsels' indulgence," he said, "I'd like to talk to the Smith-Smiths a little bit here. Bear with me a while, gentlemen."

He glanced briefly at one of the interrogatories again.

"Mr. Smith-Smith," he said.

"Yes, Your Honor?" Sylvia's father said.

"Would you mind if I just called you Mr. Smith?" the judge said. "That's not a ruling, just a request."

"Not at all, Your Honor."

"Thank you," the judge said. "Now, it says here, in response to question three, the one about who you stayed or traveled with—do you remember what you wrote?"

"I think so, Your Honor."

"Says here you once went to Chicago on business with a Mrs. Mcgillicuddy in your suitcase. Is that true?"

"Your Honor?"

"Is it true?" Sylvia's father thought a minute.

"Well, yes, Your Honor, it's true, but that's not what I wrote."

"Just talk to me a minute, though. Who, for the record, is Mrs. Mcgillicuddy?" Sylvia's father had a puzzled, almost astonished look on his face.

"That would have been my daughter's doll, Your Honor," her father said. "She hasn't had a doll in years, though, Your Honor. I mean, she's on computers now."

"Computers, you say?" the judge said, looking again at Sylvia. "I see."

"I don't understand," her father said. "Russ, what's going on here?"

"Your Honor," Russell Myers said, looking through his notes, "I'm sure both counsel would like to know . . ."

"In good time, gentlemen, please. Give me a few minutes, and I think we can clear everything up. Mr. Smith, what exactly was Mrs. Mcgillicuddy doing in your suitcase?"

"My daughter insisted that I take her. She said the doll would keep me safe. I was flying in an airplane, and Sylvia didn't understand—she got scared. She didn't know about airplanes. She said nothing could hurt Mrs. Mcgillicuddy." He looked at his lawyer and shrugged.

"And did she keep you safe?"

"Your Honor?"

"Did anything *bad* happen?"

"No sir."

"Did anything *good* happen?"

"Well," her father said, "actually, a potential client saw the doll sitting on my bed and took a liking to me. I ended up getting the account."

"This was a major account?"

"Yes, Your Honor."

"A union pension fund?"

"Yes sir. It says that there?"

"It isn't exactly sure," the judge said. Sylvia couldn't quite remember. The judge glanced at her. "It says to celebrate, you flew your wife and daughter to Chicago, and from there you drove up to a resort in Wisconsin."

"That's true. We used to live in Chicago."

"And your daughter caught a twenty-pound walleye?"

"More like five pounds, Your Honor," her father said.

Sylvia blushed in her chair. The judge smiled at her.

"Now, Mrs. Smith," the judge said, shifting his gaze.

"Your Honor," Sylvia's mother said, "I prefer to be called by my proper name, if you don't mind."

"Smith-Smith?"

"Yes, Your Honor."

The judge cocked an eyebrow in disapproval, but said nothing.

"Mrs. Smith-Smith. It says here that in the summer of eighty-two, you traveled to Europe with your daughter. Is that correct?"

"Yes, Your Honor."

"Where did you go?"

"All over, Your Honor. Paris, Rome . . ."

"Was Mrs. Mcgillicuddy along?"

"Sylvia was too old by then."

"Uh-huh," the judge said. "It says here that you burst into tears at a fountain in Rome. Is that what happened?"

"That's not what I wrote," she said. "I don't see why something I didn't write should have any bearing here."

"I know you didn't write it, but I'd like to know if it's true. I'll decide what does or doesn't have a bearing. That's my job, you know."

"I don't see how you could know about that," she said. "I never told anybody."

"Not your husband?"

Sylvia thought her mother looked like she was almost ready to cry all over again.

"No."

"Can you tell us now?" the judge said. "Is it true?"

"I suppose it's true, Your Honor," she said.

"Could you tell the court why?"

"It reminded me of something."

"What would that be?"

"I don't see how that could be important."

"It's important because I have to decide what to do with you two, and I don't even know you," the judge said. He took a drink of water and waited.

"It reminded me of a Chinese restaurant in Cambridge David and I used to eat in, when we were first going out."

"Yes?"

"There was a goldfish pond in the restaurant that people threw money in. The fountain reminded me of it, that's all."

"So," the judge said, "you and David threw money in the goldfish pond?"

"Yes."

"And what else?" the judge asked. "You might as well say it—it's all here."

"We threw everything," Sylvia's mother said. "Jewelry, money, watches—we were young and foolish. We said we didn't need anything but each other."

"And that's what made you cry—remembering that?"

"Yes."

"When you cried, did you explain it to your daughter?"

"I suppose I must have," she said.

"I see," the judge said.

"I didn't know at the time that my husband was spending the week in Boston with his girlfriend."

"Is that true, Mr. Smith?"

"No, Your Honor, it's not," David Smith-Smith said. "She was there, but she was not my girlfriend."

"That would be Miss Caldewell?"

"Yes."

"Is she your girlfriend now?"

"She's a friend," he said. "I could say she's a very good friend. We've seen each other socially since the separation, and she's helped me get through a lot of this. We talk."

"That's all?" the judge said. "Do you sleep together? I have to ask."

"No," he said. "We've discussed it, but I said I couldn't really think about it until this is over. Maybe not even then. I don't know how you can go to bed with someone you don't love. I know I don't sound normal when I say that, but it means a lot to me."

"What does?"

"Love," David Smith-Smith said. "Being together, in a bed. I never was one of those men who can sleep around. I want it to be important."

"Have you ever been unfaithful to your wife?"

"No."

"Then why does she think you have?"

"Because," he said, "because I was stupid. I wanted to make her jealous, so I told her I'd had an affair. It's a long story. Later, when I admitted I lied, she didn't believe me."

"Mrs. Smith-Smith, have you been unfaithful to your husband?"

"No, Your Honor."

"Do you believe each other?"

Sylvia's father looked at Sylvia's mother.

"Yes," he said.

"I don't know what to believe," she said.

"It says here," the judge said, "in the part about how you've attempted to reconcile, that you haven't talked to each other in six months. You had a fight in December and that was the last real time. Is that true?"

"No, Your Honor," her father said.

"Maybe we haven't been quite as . . ." her mother began.

"It says here you ask Sylvia to take messages back and forth, but that you haven't been alone with each other in a place you could talk since last winter. Is that true?"

No one spoke.

"Is it true?"

"Partially," her father said. "I mean, yes."

"Mrs. Smith-Smith?"

"Perhaps it's true," she said.

"It says here you bought your daughter a computer for her birthday, Mrs. Smith-Smith. Mr. Smith, what did you give her?"

"A computer."

"Does that sound like something that would happen to a couple that's communicating?"

"No sir."

"I agree. Would Sylvia Smith-Smith please approach the bench," the judge said. The bench itself was too high for Sylvia to see over, so the judge gestured that she come around the side. He looked at her for a few moments, and then spoke, leaning forward, in a voice just above a whisper.

"Sylvia," the judge said, "just how smart are you?"

"Well, judge," Sylvia said, "I mean, Your Honor, uh, I don't know."

"Sylvia," the judge said, "it looks to me like somebody's been using a computer to tamper with legal documents. Do you have any idea who could have done such a thing?"

"Well," Sylvia said.

"Do you know this is a fairly serious crime, Sylvia?"

"It is?" she said. "Are you going to send, you know, whoever did it, to the slammer?"

"The problem," the judge said, "in cases like this is that it's virtually impossible to trace back to the source of the tampering, after the fact."

"It is?"

"Yup. However, we can definitely nail the culprit, the next time it happens."

"I have a feeling it won't happen again," Sylvia said.

"I do, too," the judge said. He sat up in his chair. "Will all parties approach the bench please."

Sylvia's mother and father, with their lawyers, stood before the judge.

"Gentlemen," the judge said, "Madam, it seems I'm forced to declare a mistrial here, in light of the fact that your interrogatories have been altered slightly."

"May counsel see those documents, Your Honor?" Russell Myers said.

"I think I'd like to study them a little while longer," the judge said. He took his glasses off. "It's the duty of this court to exact a fair and equitable separation in marriages where an honest effort has been made to talk about the problems and see if there isn't possibly a way to work through them. I get the feeling here that such an effort has not been made. Do you agree, Mr. Smith? Mrs. Smith-Smith?"

Sylvia's parents looked at each other.

"I'm going to ask the clerk," the judge said, "to reschedule this hearing for next October."

"Your Honor, please," Sylvia's mother's lawyer said.

"I know that's a long time, Jim," the judge said, "but I'm sure you'll find something to keep you busy until then. In the meantime," he said, pointing at Sylvia's parents with his glasses, "I want you two to talk to each other. Not through your daughter. I could make that an order, but I don't think I have to. I know it's hard, but I think your marriage has enough going for it to try again. The next time I see you, I'm going to insist on seeing proof that you've tried. Okay?"

"Okay," Sylvia's father said.

"That's good," the judge said. "You might also try to keep an eye on what Sylvia's doing on her computer. I don't want to wake up some morning and read in the paper that she's gone and started World War III out of boredom."

"Yes, Your Honor," Sylvia's mother said.

"You wouldn't do that, would you Sylvia?"

"Oh, no way, judge," Sylvia said.

"I'll sleep better," the judge said. "I order the three of you to go have lunch together." He banged his gavel. "Bailiff;" he said, "would you call the next case, please?"

How Sylvia Smith-Smith
Took On the School Board
and Changed the History of
the World

The first time Sylvia Smith-Smith tried to fight city hall, she had only common sense, human decency, and the spirit of Christmas on her side. She thought that those three combined with the hip-to-toe cast on her right leg, her natural above-average ability to charm people—by hook or by crook—wit, intelligence, and the sheer obduracy a precocious only child develops from instinct should have been enough. The occasion was a hearing of the school board's subcommittee on disciplinary actions, a three-person panel chaired by a man named David West. The hearing would decide whether or not Sylvia would flunk all her classes for the semester, a punishment she didn't feel she deserved.

"Is a Miss Smith present?" the chairman asked. He was Dan Quayle–ish, forty, blond, with red-rimmed glasses.

"It's Smith-Smith," Sylvia said, rising from her

seat. She could have stood without her crutches, but she grabbed them for effect. She was wearing a blue denim skirt and a navy sweatshirt, all against the advice of Mr. Potter, her guidance counselor, who'd suggested she dress to make a good impression. She'd refused, arguing that she was going to a hearing, not a fashion show. Her friend Marcie was seated on one side of her, Sylvia's father on the other side. There were only six other people in the room, which included a young woman with a notepad who Sylvia assumed was a reporter. "With a hyphen. My mother's maiden name was the same as my father's, but she refused to take his name."

"I see," David West said, not smiling. If this guy didn't have a sense of humor, Sylvia knew she could be in trouble. He scanned a sheet of paper in a manila folder in front of him, as did the other two members of the panel—a man named Mr. Vasquez and an older woman named Mrs. Thompson. "You are a student at Weston High School?" he asked, not looking up.

"Yup," Sylvia said.

He looked up. Maybe she should have said "Yes, sir."

"It says here you've missed seven days of school," he continued. "November twenty-first, twenty-second, twenty-third, twenty-eighth, twenty-ninth, thirtieth and December eighth—correct?"

"That is correct." Sylvia said. "I'd like to explain."

"That's what you're here for," the chairman said. He smiled at her, though she didn't think he meant it. He glanced at his watch. "Why don't you tell us why you're appealing Principal Brickman's ruling, and we'll discuss the rest of it later. Start by explaining where you were on those days."

"Well," Sylvia began, "from the twentieth to the twenty-third, I was skiing in Breckenridge, Colorado." The main reason for the ski trip was that it was a rare chance for the Smith-Smith family to be together. Sylvia's parents had been separated for over a year. It seemed important to Sylvia to go, even though she'd never skied before and didn't really want to learn. "It was the only time my whole family could get away. I got written permission from all my teachers, who said I could make up the work I missed and take make-up tests when I got back. I even studied in the chalet at night when everybody else was having fun."

"I can attest to that," her father said, half rising from his seat.

"That she was studying, or that everybody else was having fun?" Mrs. Thompson asked.

"That I was studying," Sylvia said. "Mr. Brickman signed my permission slip too."

"This slip?" David West asked, waving a piece of paper in the air. He read the note, flaring his nostrils the way Earl the Brickhead had when he'd read it. Brickman was called "Brickhead" because of his name, but mostly because he was bald, which—combined with the white shirt he always wore (sleeves rolled up) and bow tie—made him look a bit like an ice-cream vendor. He was also "The Brickhead" because, although it was his first year at Weston, he was already known to have the intellectual flexibility of a brick, but not quite the personality. He fancied himself *tough but fair*. True enough, in that he was *unfair* to everyone equally, and if you didn't like it, *tough*. Students were describing his first semester as the "reign of terror." Sylvia had dreaded going in to see him, and she was one of the best students in school.

"You were skiing while the other students were in class?" Mr. Vasquez asked.

"Well, yes, but as I mentioned earlier—"

"It says here," the chairman interrupted, "that Mr. Brickman explained to you the conflict with school policy."

"You are aware, are you not," Brickhead had said, in an utterly patronizing tone, "that any student who misses more than six days per grading period automatically receives failing grades in all his or her classes? If I excuse you from classes, it doesn't mean you're exempt from school policy." Don't treat me like a unique individual, she'd thought at the time.

"He did," Sylvia replied, "but it was only supposed to be Monday through Wednesday. After that was Thanksgiving vacation."

"What about the other days you missed?" West asked.

"Well, as you can see," Sylvia said, shifting on her crutches and wincing, "I have a broken leg, which I broke on Sunday." She'd been skiing down the Bunny Hills all week and decided to try an intermediate hill for a change. From the top of the slope, she'd spotted her mother and father standing in front of the chalet, and thought it would be fun to ski down to them. She thought she'd learned enough to snowplow to a stop right beside them. She thought wrong, hit the chalet at about twenty miles an hour, and broke her right tibia in two places. Stupid place to put a building anyway. "The twenty-eighth, I was in the hospital. The twenty-ninth, we flew home, and the thirtieth, it still hurt too much to put any weight on it. The thirty-first, it still hurt, but I couldn't miss any more school—so I came anyway."

She exchanged glances with Marcie, who gave her the thumbs-up sign.

"There are only thirty days in November," David West corrected her, making it sound as if he'd caught her in a lie. "But you're saying you were fully aware that you'd reached your limit of absences? You knew that since only three of your absences were medically excused, and the other three were unexempted, another absence meant you'd receive failing grades?"

"I don't know if I'd say I was *fully* aware," Sylvia said, trying to seem self-effacing. "But, yes, I guess I knew."

"How did you miss the seventh day?" Mrs. Thompson asked.

"I broke my leg again," Sylvia said. At the class Snow Party, an annual event held at a nearby golf course—mostly tobogganing, dancing, and snowball fights. Stupid Richie Kingsbury tried to impress Marcie, whom he'd had a crush on since eighth grade, by sliding down the hill with a paper bag over his head. Sylvia was standing next to Marcie when Richie Kingsbury hit a bump, sending him flying in Sylvia's direction. Before she could move or even scream, he hit them, knocking both Sylvia and Marcie over like bowling pins. Marcie was a little shaken up. Sylvia refractured her leg for the second time in three weeks.

The panel conferred for a few moments, switching

off their microphones. David West glanced at his watch again, which Sylvia knew was not a good sign. She had a bad feeling. Nobody was laughing at her jokes, for one thing.

"Why do you think we should make an exception for you?" the chairman finally asked. "It seems clear you knew the policy, were warned of the consequences, took the risk anyway, and broke the rule. You're not denying that, are you?"

"No, I'm not denying it," Sylvia said, getting a little hot under the collar. "If we'd lied in the first place and pretended I was out sick instead of out skiing, I wouldn't even be here. I'm being honest. I'm only saying I feel you should make an exception because I don't think the policy applies to me. The rule exists to keep students in school. You want students kept in school so that they can learn. As you can see, I learned everything I would have learned if I hadn't missed school. I had straight A's before I left, and I got A's on all my make-up tests when I got back. If you have my record there, you'll see that in three years I've never skipped a class or missed a single day except when I had mono. I'm a hard worker. Giving me F's won't accurately reflect my performance in class, or give a true indication of what I've learned. In the long run it will only undermine the credibility of everyone else's grades." She'd worked on that one the night before. "I just don't think it would be fair to flunk me, especially since I'm going to be applying to colleges soon and the grades this semester are the ones they're going to look at."

Sylvia sat down. The panel conferred again. Sylvia studied their faces. Thompson seemed irritated, Vasquez indifferent, West harried and pressed for time. The conference ended when Vasquez shrugged, Mrs. Thompson nodded, and David West spun in his swivel chair. They couldn't have discussed the issue for more than half a minute.

"Miss Smith-Smith," the chairman began, clearing away the papers in front of him and making a note on the manila folder, "we find it, first of all, lamentable that you broke your leg, and in that regard, we're sorry. We also find it commendable that you seem to be an industrious student and that your previous record is above average in most respects."

Sylvia knew from his tone of voice what his next word would be.

"However—"

That was it.

"We want to impress on you that school is more than just learning material. It's learning how to be a good citizen as well, and how to be part of your community. Just because you're a good student doesn't mean you only go to school when you feel like it. The poorer students in your classes benefit from your presence too, don't forget. Students learn from each other as well as from their teachers. For the main, school is learning that to get along in society you have to respect and obey rules. That goes for straight-A students and C students and D students alike. I'm afraid the decision stands and the appeal is denied."

"Come on, slug-a-bed," her mother said. "It's six-thirty."

Sylvia kept her eyes closed and said nothing. Her leg

ached. Her stomach ached, still knotted up from the night before. She didn't like depression, and had only really felt it after her dog Betsy died. Through her parents' separation, through all the fights, the emotional and physical dislocations, she'd always stayed optimistic, cheerfully pessimistic at the very least, either pulled forward by a belief in the future or realistically resigned to her fate. Now she felt only black and empty inside. Not just that everything was out of control—it was out of control and she didn't care. It wasn't that long ago when life seemed simple. You brushed your teeth, said your prayers, did your homework, fed your pets, treated your friends right, and everything turned out fine. It seemed like nothing had gone right since the day they fired Jane Pauley.

"Come on Syl—time for school." Her mother's voice sounded flat and distant. Sylvia didn't want to answer.

"Sylvia—" Her mother waited.

"What's the point?" she said at last. "I've already flunked."

Her mother gently rubbed her back, the way she rubbed it when Sylvia was sick. She was wearing her old quilted bathrobe.

"Maybe you should go just because you've never been a quitter," her mother said. She raised the window shade, then sat back down on the edge of the bed. The day was only beginning to lighten—it would be another overcast December morning.

"I'm one now," Sylvia said. She meant it. She rolled over. Suddenly she hated the house where she and her mother lived, the stupid texturings in the ceiling plaster, the cold-flow distortion in the window glass.

"So they win then?" her mother asked.

"Right," Sylvia said. "They win. Go away."

"Now you want to take it out on me?" her mother asked. Sylvia stared out the window. The sky was gray and lumpy, like the color of Brickhead's heart. She pictured him in his office waiting for school to begin by making paper-clip chains and plotting whose life he'd ruin that day.

"Do you remember the story your father used to tell you about the mouse and the rattlesnake?"

A simple fable. A rattlesnake, lurking outside a mouse hole, caught a mouse coming out. There was no escape for the mouse, no last minute reprieve. Did the mouse quit? Instead of giving up, he ran down to the far end of the rattlesnake and shook the snake's rattle so loud that the other mice heard it and ran to safety. The moral: *Even when you're doomed, make some noise.*

"You used to like that story."

"I remember," Sylvia said. "I always wondered why the mouse wasn't paralyzed by the snake's venom."

"If you want to be paralyzed, fine," her mother said, losing patience. "Stay home, but if you do you'll ruin any chance of a second appeal."

Sylvia did have that right, if she wanted to take her case before the whole thirteen-person school board, which met the following Monday. She felt so defeated already that it seemed a lost cause, but then again, there was no point in closing off her options prematurely. She began to get dressed.

She walked around school that day like a zombie. A few students talked about organizing a protest on her behalf, but she knew nothing would come of it. She fantasized about walking into Brickhead's office and doing something she'd really regret, like apologizing and throwing herself at his feet. Mostly she sulked and didn't begin to snap out of her funk until she got home, to find a message waiting for her on the answering machine to call someone named Rachel Burns, a reporter for the local paper. She wanted to do a story on Sylvia, explaining that the school board was part of her regular beat.

"I was at the meeting last night, sitting in the corner," Rachel Burns explained. "I should have talked to you then, but I had to run."

"Why me?" Sylvia said. "What good would it do?"

"Probably none," Burns said, "except I think you're getting screwed, and that's always a good read." Sylvia told her the whole story, from the beginning, and gave her the names of corroborating witnesses—Marcie and Richie Kingsbury. The reporter's last question had Sylvia baffled.

"So what are you going to do next?"

"Nothing, I guess," Sylvia said. "Can't fight city hall, right?"

"Actually, it's easier than you think," the reporter said. "I do it every day. And if you don't mind my saying so, you went about it all wrong."

"How?"

"You tried to buck the system, instead of using it to your advantage," she said. "You should think of bureaucracy as a play in which everybody acts his or her part, but nobody's read the entire play. All you have to do is read the whole play. Read *all* the rules because every bureaucracy has a million rules, and whoever knows what they are has the most power. You can't change the rules, but you don't want to because usually you can use their own rules against them. Most people never know where to begin, so they just throw up their hands and say, 'Oh well—can't fight city hall.'"

Sylvia knew that a big part of her depression was not knowing what to do next.

"Where *do* I begin?" Sylvia asked.

"Have you got access to a computer with a modem?"

"Right here in my bedroom," Sylvia said.

"Then you might begin with P.A.I.N.," the reporter said. "Public Access Information Network. This is one of the few towns where most public records have been put into a computer data base. You can dial in and get city ordinances, school-board minutes, whatever you want, going back twenty years. If you have a few computer skills, you'll be amazed what you can find out."

"Maybe I'll try," Sylvia said. She had nothing better to do.

"One more thing," Rachel Burns said. "If you do go up in front of the school board, dress up. Maybe it's stupid, but it's important-stupid."

Sylvia spent that week, after school and at night after supper, plugged into the Public Access Information Network. It was even better than going down to the Hall of Records because the Hall of Records closed at five-thirty, but P.A.I.N. stayed open until one in the morning. Probably for lawyers burning the midnight oil. Each day proved more interesting than the one before. On the first day she scanned the school committee bylaws. On the second, she pored over the committee meeting minutes for the previous ten years, not reading every word, of course, but searching for specific references. The beauty of running a computer search was that the machine could sift through thousands of pages of documents and flag every mention of a specific name. Earl T. Brickman, for instance. Or specific words—*absenteeism* or *truancy* —or even cross index. By the third day, she knew she was onto something. She searched the personnel files, boning up on the members of the school board, their careers and histories. After the personnel files, she searched titles and deeds, the public records that told who owned the properties and businesses in town. She even searched wedding, birth, and death records, directing her computer to sift out anything that might be of use to her. When she was finished, she printed her results in a report. She printed out a second copy and mailed it to Rachel Burns under the melodramatic heading *"To Be Opened in the Event of My Death."* She made a third copy to give to Elliot Ford, the superintendant of schools. By Monday night she was again feeling confident and ready to make some noise. The second time Sylvia Smith-Smith tried to fight city hall, she had more than charm, wit, common sense, human decency, and the spirit of Christmas on her side—she had the law.

Better than that. She had the dirt.

"The chair recognizes Miss—Smith, is it?" the chairperson said. His name was Clifford Durganis, district supervisor, answerable to Elliot Ford.

It was near the end of the evening. Durganis shuffled papers a little impatiently. "You know, the sub-committee has already ruled on your appeal of Principal Brickman's decision." Sylvia turned to see Brickman seated at the back of the room. She'd written him a note asking that he be there, and was a little surprised to see that he'd obliged. "Unless you have some new information, I really don't think we can afford to spend too much more time on this."

"I do, your honor," Sylvia said, standing. "Have new information, that is." She was wearing her mother's best suit, charcoal pinstripes, with a white blouse and pearls. She felt she looked about fifty. Her hair was pulled back and held in a silver barrette, rendering her lawyer-ish, severe and professional. She felt foolish, but then, this was their game, not hers. She was even wearing panty hose, albeit only on one leg; the other had to be tied around her cast.

Durganis smiled. "You don't have to call me 'your honor.' I'm not a judge," he said. "All right then, but keep it brief."

"I'd like to request a closed-door meeting."

Durganis smiled again. "This isn't Perry Mason," the chairman told her. "It's a public hearing. Just go ahead and say what you have to say."

Exactly the answer Sylvia had hoped for.

"Okay," Sylvia said, taking her report out of her briefcase. "First of all, I guess I should say that according to my research, the school district's attendance policy, the one affecting me, which states that six absences constitutes a failing grade, was proposed on April 19, 1987, by a David West—is that correct?"

David West nodded, amused at this upstart girl.

"According to the minutes of that meeting, Mr.

West's motion was never seconded. According to school-board bylaws, section two, paragraph four, as well as according to *Robert's Rules of Order,* a motion cannot be carried unless it has been seconded. The policy is therefore invalid."

There were a good twenty or thirty onlookers in the room, all of whom were suddenly silent. Durganis conferred with the man seated next to him.

"That's an interesting bit of research you've done, young lady," he said, "but I'm sure it's just an oversight. It was probably seconded."

Sylvia noticed a woman scribbling in a notepad. Rachel Burns.

"It's not in the minutes," Sylvia said, "so it can't be assumed. Furthermore, it is also stated in the school-board bylaws, section fifteen, paragraph twelve, that no person shall be allowed to serve as a school committee member of this district unless he or she is a resident of this district. The public records show that Mr. West, now residing at One-twelve Sixteenth Street, which is in the district, was living at Fourteen twenty-eight Westbrook Road on April 19, 1987. The Westbrook Road house is not in the district. He didn't close on the Sixteenth Street house until July. Therefore, he was not eligible to propose the motion in the first place."

Durganis whispered something to David West, then to another man seated on his right.

"Maybe we should meet in closed session, after all," he said. "All these matters concerning residency are beyond the province of this—"

"You can't," Sylvia said. "Section three, paragraph ten states that once a session has been declared open it must remain open—closed-door sessions can only be scheduled for a later date." Durganis's expression was one of dismay. "Anyway, if I may continue," Sylvia said, "I've also learned that when the school district boundaries were redrawn in 1988, it was determined that the easternmost boundary of the district would be set at the center of Sperry Boulevard. Since Mrs. Thompson, currently seated on the board, lives on the east side of that street, the 1988 redistricting disqualifies her from serving as well."

Durganis banged his gavel.

"That's not relevant to your appeal, Miss Smith," the chairman said. "We will take your comments under advisement."

"It's relevant because she denied my first appeal," Sylvia said. "Besides, I'm not finished."

"Oh yes you are," the chairman said.

"Let her speak," Rachel Burns said. "It's a public hearing."

"You have to let me speak," Sylvia said. "Section three, paragraph fourteen."

There was much whispering among the school committee members as they tried to decide what to do to get rid of Sylvia. Finally several of them nodded.

"Upon further review, and in light of the evidence you've turned up regarding possible irregularities in the way the school attendance policy was drafted and enacted," the chairman said, "the board has decided to reverse Principal Brickman's ruling. You've made your case, Miss Smith."

"Good," Sylvia said, smiling. "But I'm still not finished." She turned the page in her report. "For instance, I think it should be read into the minutes that when Mr. Earl T. Brickman was appointed principal of Weston High School last summer—and by the way, it seems only fair to add that when Mr. Brickman was a senior at Central in 1966, according to his school records he had twenty-eight unexcused absences and a grade-point average two point three points below mine—anyway, when he was appointed principal, his previous experience consisted only of teaching five years of shop at Vocational Tech and two years of seventh grade English. The bylaws recommend that the school committee not appoint anyone principal with less than fifteen years experience teaching, and/or ten years teaching and five years administrative experience. In fact, the current district supervisor, Mr. Durganis, has made four appointments and only one appointee has fifteen years experience. One has eight, and the other only three. By your own rules, these people are not qualified."

A murmur went up. Durganis seemed resigned to letting Sylvia finish.

"I won't even mention that no women or minorities have been appointed. In addition to that, one of the appointees, Mr. Joseph Rippucci, principal at Kennedy High School, was for ten years, while a teacher, also a business partner of Chairman Durganis's brother at East Side Realty, in which the chairman has a twenty percent interest. Mr. Rippucci, in fact, sold Mr. Durganis his house. Another appointee, Mr. Kevin Clark, the principal at Jefferson, was also a former business partner of Mr. West. They owned a construction company called West and Associates, now called A and L Architectural Contracting, run by Mr. West's brother-in-law. Finally, Mr. Brickman, according to public records, was the witness at Mr. Durganis's wedding, and they both graduated from the same college in 1970. This suggests a degree of patronage and cronyism in school-board appointments warranting further investigation."

"I'm going to call a recess," Durganis said, rapping his gavel.

"No, you aren't," Sylvia said. "I'm not finished. For anyone who may be interested, I have also uncovered and documented eleven cases where school budget money has gone to vendors, service or construction companies owned by or connected to school committee family members or associates, including twelve million dollars in contracts to A and L Architectural Contracting last year for new construction and remodeling. This included new oak paneling in Mr. Clark's office and, believe it or not, a sauna in the teacher's lounge at Central. There are probably more instances, but I ran out of time to search for them. I'll just stop there, but you should know I sent a copy of my report to the newspaper and another to the superintendent."

Afterward, Rachel Burns told Sylvia that if she wanted a job as an investigative reporter, she could start the next day. Ms. Burns said she'd have to rewrite the story she was doing on Sylvia, but she didn't mind, because she liked happy endings.

"No P.A.I.N., no gain, right?" Sylvia said.

On her way out the door, she noticed Principal Brickman. She approached him cautiously.

"Hello, Mr. Brickman," Sylvia said, trying not to gloat. "How'd I do?"

He paused before speaking.

"That was brilliant," he said. His praise took Sylvia completely by surprise. "Congratulations. Where on earth did you learn all those things?"

"It was all in the public record," she said, still stunned. "I used my computer." She'd expected him to be mad. She'd hoped she might even get him fired. To hear him congratulating her seemed completely out of character.

"Well, I think you did a fabulous job researching your case," he said.

"You're not mad?"

"I suppose I'm a little put off at having my credentials challenged, but I'm sure they'll stand up under further scrutiny. I actually have another seven years teaching in California that you didn't mention."

"Oh," Sylvia said. "I'm sorry."

"It's all right," he said. "As for cronyism, it's true I was the witness at Cliff's wedding, but I was a friend of his wife. Cliff and I had a falling out when he and Sharon got divorced ten years ago. We've barely spoken since. I was appointed principal over his objections."

"I didn't know," Sylvia said.

"I'm sure you didn't," Brickman said. "At any rate, the rest of your presentation was truly remarkable. That conflict of interest stuff was dynamite. It should make things very interesting around here for quite some time. I do think it was mostly luck that got your grades restored, but you went at it through due process, so it's a decision we can all live with."

Sylvia smiled. This man she'd disliked so much was almost likable.

"You were only doing what you had to," she found herself saying.

"I really am responsible for applying policy evenly," he said. "I can't make exceptions. It was funny when you mentioned all my own absences. I was practically a juvenile delinquent in high school. A typical long-haired hippie. I even got busted a couple times, just between you and me, but that was erased from my record because I kept my nose clean after that. Scared straight, you could say."

Brickman a long-haired hippie? It staggered the imagination.

"Maybe it's because I learned the hard way that I'm a bit zealous about rules. But as we've seen, in a roundabout way, I think you've learned just how useful rules are."

"I guess so," Sylvia said. "It just felt important to me to remember that no matter what the rules are, people are still individuals." Her father was beckoning from the doorway. He'd promised to take her out for ice cream. "Including high school principals, I suppose."

"I take that as a compliment," he said. "Just don't let the word get out that old Brickhead's gone soft or it'll be anarchy at Weston."

"You know about your nickname?" Sylvia asked.

"I've been called Brickhead since sixth grade," he said. "I've gotten to where I sort of like it."

"I won't tell anyone," she said. "Though I don't think it would mean anarchy at Weston if people knew you aren't as tough as you look."

She didn't tell anyone either, though word did begin

to spread at Weston High School that Mr. Brickman wasn't such a bad guy. The rumor started (and the "reign of terror" ended) when Marcie noticed and pointed out to everyone at school, that Mr. Brickman had signed Sylvia's cast. A forgery, Sylvia claimed. But not too adamantly.

JTK LVS SSS

YOU ARE DEFINITELY CUTE.

Those were the words, right in the middle of Sylvia's monitor, signed JTK. What would summer be, without a little romance? More relaxing, that's what it would be.

First, Sylvia thought the computer was getting fresh. It was more than a little cute. It was her third day at Campion College Computer Camp, but it still surprised her, each time she logged on in the morning, when the computer greeted her with a HI CAMPER-- HOW WERE YOUR EGGS THIS MORNING? The computer's name was Cecil, though, for Campion College Linear. Who was JTK?

"Okay, guys," Virginia, their instructor-counselor said, pointing at them with a long piece of chalk, "this is supposed to be an advanced class, but we lack fluency . . ."

Sylvia daydreamed. She was only now getting used

to the idea that she was in camp again. She hadn't been to one since she was eleven. She didn't golf, or sail, or play volleyball, or tennis, or tie square knots, or rope deer, or build igloos out of birch trees or any of the things they made you do at camps. Camps were places popular with outdoorsy types, younger kids, granolas, crazed grizzly bears and mass-murdering madmen recently escaped from insane asylums near-by, with nothing better to do than terrorize helpless Girl Scouts. The first part of the summer had been so nice. She would have preferred to stay home and write short stories, do something constructive, or just hang out, but her mother was going to Arizona for a month, which meant Sylvia would have had to either go with her or stay with her father. She couldn't decide which would be more unpleasant, Arizona or Manhattan in midsummer. The computer camp was accredited, and credits from advanced classes would transfer to col-lege. Sylvia had just started on computers that spring and knew she was behind a lot of the other kids she'd be competing with in college. It would be good to get better at them. But still. Camp.

WHAT AM I DOING HERE, CECIL?

JUST DO THE BEST YOU CAN.

BUT WHAT ABOUT THE GRIZZLY BEARS ES-CAPED FROM INSANE ASYLUMS WITH AXES THE SIZE OF SAILBOAT RUDDERS?

HAVE NO FEAR. JTK WILL PROTECT YOU.

For the second time, Sylvia was shocked.

WHO IS JTK?

WOULDN'T YOU LIKE TO KNOW? JTK.

Sylvia glanced quickly around the lab. Virginia was

still talking, and as far as she could tell, everybody was listening. The evidence was clear. Someone, calling himself JTK, was raiding her program. A wise guy, eh?

"I think it's romantic," one of Sylvia's roommates, Sandra, said that night after evening free time. All the campers lived in one dorm, near the lake, boys in the north wing, girls in the south. Older students had the top floors. Ages at camp ranged from seventh grade to twelfth. Sylvia and her three roommates had a quad, a large room with two bunk beds in it. They were in the third-floor lounge, making popcorn. Sylvia had worried about getting along with them, but they seemed okay. She wore a bathrobe and beach thongs.

"I agree," Jodie said, stuffing popcorn into her face.

"Oh God," Sylvia said, "I think it's insipid."

"Hungry, Jodie?" Allexis said, a tall thin girl from Boston, slightly spoiled, Sylvia thought—she'd brought her own DEC Rainbow from home.

"Oh come off it, Allexis, I saw you hoovering down Jell-O at dinner," Sandra said.

"That was Jell-O?" Sylvia said. "I thought it was meatloaf."

"You don't *hoover* with your mouth, stupid, you *hoover* with your nose," Allexis said.

"I'm glad we have an expert in the terminology of drug abuse here," Sandra said.

"Besides," Allexis said, "there aren't any calories in Jell-O."

"There aren't any in popcorn, either," Jodie said, shoveling in another handful.

"There's calories in the butter," Allexis said.

"We don't have any butter, bird brain," Sandra said.

"I still think it's romantic," Jodie said.

"It's stupid," Sylvia said. "It's an invasion of my privacy. If someone likes me, why don't they just come up to me and tell me? This is junior high school stuff."

"Maybe he's a seventh grader," Allexis said.

"You don't have to be young to be awkward, if you're a boy," Jodie said. "There was a guy yesterday who was trying to impress that blonde from California by showing her he could eat ten hamburgers, and he got so sick he barfed."

"Was she impressed?" Sandra said.

"I would be," Sylvia said.

"I've seen about three guys who barely begin to impress me," Allexis said. "The rest are all nerds. Of course, what do you expect from a computer camp? They'd all be nerds."

"What does that make us?" Jodie said.

"I don't know," Sandra said. "I admire brains in a boy."

"Because it's so rare," Sylvia said.

"There must be *some* interesting guys here," Jodie said. "I don't care if they're smart, so long as they're . . ."

"Experienced," Allexis said.

"Yeah," Sandra said. "Have you ever known any experienced boys, Sylvia?"

"Well," Sylvia said. "I went to the prom with a married man, but that's a long story." Her roommates were appropriately shocked. She told them briefly about David.

"But you're not, like, going together now or anything, are you?" Sandra said. Sylvia shook her head. "So you're, like, free and available, right?"

"I suppose so," Sylvia said. "It's not exactly what I came here looking to find."

"It found you, remember?" Allexis said. "JTK. Jonathan Tillingsworth Kennington."

"Jack Tumor-face Kingkong," Jodie said. Everyone laughed.

"We need a test," Allexis declared.

"What?" Sandra said.

"You know," Allexis said. "One of those 'what's your love-quotient' tests, like they have in *Cosmopolitan* all the time. Oh yes! We can even use it as a project. We'll make everybody take it, and then we'll know which boys are the good ones. We can use my DEC."

"How much money should a gentleman spend on a woman?" Jodie said. "Four, five or six hundred dollars in an evening."

"Women are always right, true or false," Sandra said. "Oh let's." They rose to go.

"This is definitely junior high stuff now," Sylvia said.

"Oh come on," Jodie said. "It'll be fun. Camp high jinks and all that."

"Include me out," Sylvia said.

Sylvia stayed in the lounge and read, until Virginia stuck her head in the door to inform her it was after lights-out. Sylvia returned to her room, got into bed and lay on her back for a few minutes. Her roommates were asleep, but she wasn't tired. She took a floppy disk out of her suitcase and tiptoed down the hall barefoot, closing the lounge door silently behind her. Each lounge had a Commodore SuperPet in it, networked to the college computer, for the kids to use during free time.

HI, SYLVIA. YOU'RE UP LATE.

HI, CECIL. WHO IS JTK?

NO NAME IN FILE. SORRY.

OKAY. GO TO FLOPPY PLEASE.

Cecil did as she asked. Sylvia looked out the window, at the full moon that hung over the lake like a night-light.

DAY THREE

DEAR DIARY,

A BOY LIKES ME. I SWOON, I SWOON. HONESTLY. MAMA DONE TOLD ME THIS WOULD HAPPEN. SHE DIDN'T SAY IT WOULD BE A SECRET ADMIRER WHO HAS FOUND A WAY TO INVADE MY PROGRAM AND LEAVE MESSAGES. WHY MUST BOYS PLAY GAMES LIKE THIS? IT'S SO IMMATURE. EVEN DAVID PLAYED GAMES, IN HIS WAY. I DON'T THINK I WANT THIS, NOT HERE OR NOT NOW. BUT THEN I SAY TO MYSELF, WHY NOT? WHAT'S THE BIG DEAL.

TOO PICKY? AFRAID? IF SO, OF WHAT? BE HONEST WITH YOURSELF.

THE ROOMMATE SITUATION IS BETTER THAN EXPECTED. SANDRA SAYS "LIKE" TOO MUCH (LIKE, ALL THE, LIKE, TIME), JODIE IS OVERWEIGHT AND WEARS TOO MUCH

MAKEUP AND ALLEXIS IS AN ANOREXIC J.A.P. SNOB. AT LEAST THOSE WERE FIRST IMPRESSIONS. BEING AN ONLY CHILD SPOILS YOU. IT'S SO ODD TO ROOM WITH OTHER PEOPLE--YOU FORGET HOW TO BE-COME INTIMATE WITH SOMEONE. ACTUALLY, THEY ARE GREAT FUN. ALLEXIS HAS A WON-DERFUL, DRY SENSE OF HUMOR AND IS RE-ALLY NICE, EVEN THOUGH SOMETIMES SHE TRIES TO HIDE IT AND BE COOL. SANDRA IS HILARIOUS AND EXTREMELY PRETTY. JODIE IS ALSO PRETTY, MAYBE THE SMARTEST ONE.

ALL IN ALL, CAMP IS OKAY. MAYBE I CAN LEARN TO BE OUTDOORSY AND SURPRISE MOM. I WOULD HAVE TO SAY MY BIGGEST DISAPPOINTMENT, SO FAR, IS THAT THERE ARE NO KILLER GRIZZLIES ESCAPED FROM INSANE ASYLUMS. WHAT KIND OF CAMP IS THIS? I WANT MY MONEY BACK.

I AM TIRED, FINALLY. SEE YOU LATER.

Sylvia stared at her words and yawned. She was so tired she could barely keep her eyes open.

The next morning after the bell sounded to wake everybody up, Virginia knocked on the door and handed Sylvia her floppy, saying she must have left it in the machine. Sylvia made a mental note to be more careful.

In morning lab, there was a new development. Cecil's cheerful HI CAMPER--HOW WAS YOUR BREAK-FAST? was replaced by a graphic of a death skull and the words, I AM GOR! GOR RULES THE K. CECIL IS DEAD--LONG LIVE GOR! Nothing anyone did could make the skull go away. It was more of an annoyance than anything really harmful, but it took Virginia and Phil, another counselor, nearly half an hour to erase GOR's graffiti. To do so, they had to recompile the initial program load.

"People," Virginia said, once the repairs were made, "please have a seat. This, if anybody cares to know, was a very stupid and inconsiderate prank. Whoever is doing this may think it's no worse than erasing a blackboard, but illicit hacking is a crime. If anybody knows anything, please come see me, so we can talk to whoever thinks they're being cute."

Sylvia found Virginia after lunch and told her about JTK. With Cecil, they went through the camp roster in Virginia's office.

"Some of these kids are incredibly precocious," Virginia said. "Cecil is an IBM 370, so whoever's compromising it would have to speak PASCAL. You wouldn't know PASCAL, would you?"

"Is he an exchange student?" Sylvia said. "Joking. No."

Out of 206 kids in camp, eight had last names beginning with K, thirty-six first names beginning with J. Virginia told Sylvia to keep her ears open.

Sylvia was fifteen minutes late for 1:30 lab. When she logged on, there was a message for her.

YOU'RE TARDY.

I KNOW, CECIL. SORRY.

YOU'RE STILL CUTE, THOUGH.

JTK?

Sylvia looked around the room.

NONE OTHER. HOW WAS YOUR LUNCH, BY THE WAY?

NONE OF YOUR BUSINESS. THAT WAS INCREDIBLY RUDE THIS MORNING.

WHAT DID I DO?

THE COUNSELOR SAYS YOU COST THE SCHOOL A TON OF MONEY IN LOST TIME. PERSONALLY, I THINK IT'S COMPLETELY CHILDISH, GOR!

WHO IS GOR? I'M JTK, SAVIOR OF THE UNIVERSE, DEFENDER OF THE EARTH AND LORD HIGH LIGHTMASTER OF THE DARK KINGDOM.

OH NO. ARE YOU A DUNGEON-HEAD?

MAYBE.

I HATE COMPUTER GAMES.

WHY HATE THE FUTURE? THERE'S NO PERCENTAGE IN THAT.

YOU'RE NOT GOR? TELL THE TRUTH.

JTK CANNOT LIE. NO. IF I WAS DISHONEST, WHY DON'T I PRETEND I'M CECIL AND FREAK EVERYBODY OUT?

WHY DON'T YOU?

BECAUSE I'M JTK, SAVIOR OF THE UNIVERSE, DEFENDER OF THE EARTH AND LORD HIGH LIGHTMASTER OF THE DARK KINGDOM.

WHO IS GOR, THEN? HOW CAN HE SNEAK AROUND INSIDE AN IBM 370?

IT ISN'T HARD, REALLY, ONCE YOU KNOW HOW.

HOW DO YOU KNOW HOW?

WOULDN'T YOU LIKE TO KNOW?

LOOK--WHO ARE YOU, AND WHY ARE YOU BOTHERING ME?

Sylvia was angry. They called it "flaming" when people swore at each other or used foul language in a computer. Something about how it allowed you to remain anonymous freed people from the usual restraints of good manners. She felt tempted. There was a ten-second pause.

I'M SORRY.

Sylvia's screen went blank. She logged back on.

HELLO, SYLVIA--HOW WAS YOUR LUNCH?

BUG OFF, CECIL. JTK?

NO NAME IN FILE, SORRY.

JTK--I KNOW YOU'RE MONITORING ME. COME BACK. YOU'RE NOT BOTHERING ME.

No reply.

PLEASE, JTK? WE NEED YOUR HELP.

No reply.

DAMSEL IN DISTRESS.

REALLY?

YES. JUST TELL ME SOMETHING. ARE YOU A GENIUS? COMPUTERWISE?

MAYBE.

CAN YOU FIND GOR? WE NEED HELP. IF YOU KNOW HOW TO HACK, MAYBE YOU'LL BE THE BEST PERSON TO CATCH HIM.

NO SWEAT. LOG ON TONIGHT AT MIDNIGHT WITH (FGN?DID!)

SPEAK ENGLISH.

JUST DO IT. I'LL TALK TO YOU AT MIDNIGHT.

After afternoon rec time came computer free time, which usually meant games. Allexis, Jodie and Sandra had set up the love test they'd devised on the lab's twenty-four terminals. They called it the Campion College Computer Camp Personality Profile, CCCCPP for short. Virginia said it was all right, as long as no one was forced to take it, and as long as no one signed their names. The contents, she said, were no racier than your average Phil Donahue show. Allexis declared the CCCCPPs strictly optional. However, anybody refusing to take it was to be automatically labeled uncool. It also helped that no names were required. Their plan was to read the boys' tests, weed out the good ones and then try to deduce who specifically were the coolest ones by logic, age, where they said they were from and so on.

CAMPION COLLEGE COMPUTER CAMP
PERSONALITY PROFILE

PERSONAL INFORMATION:
(TELL THE TRUTH OR ELSE BE DISQUALIFIED.)

SEX_____
AGE_____
VIRGINITY YES__NO__(AGE OF LOSS, IF NO__)
NUMBER OF PAST GIRLFRIENDS OR BOYFRIENDS__

AGE OF FIRST KISS_____
HEIGHT_____
WEIGHT_____
COLOR OF EYES_____

GENERAL KNOWLEDGE

  1. A MARTINI IS MADE WITH:
    A. SCOTCH

   B. GIN
   C. BOURBON
   D. LEMONADE

2. TRUE OR FALSE: POPCORN HAS CALORIES. T F

3. TRUE OR FALSE: JELL-O HAS CALORIES. T F

4. I DO_____ DO NOT_____SMOKE CIGARETTES.

5. RANK THESE PEOPLE IN ORDER OF COOLNESS:
   A. TOM PETTY
   B. SEAN PENN
   C. ADAM ANT
   D. DAVID BYRNE
   E. MATTHEW STAR
   F. DAVID BOWIE
   G. DAVID LETTERMAN
   H. PAUL SCHAEFFER

   A. VICTORIA PRINCIPAL
   B. MARIE OSMOND
   C. STEVIE NICKS
   D. JESSICA LANGE
   E. LAURIE ANDERSON
   F. MOLLY RINGWALD
   G. MARTHA QUINN
   H. BROOKE SHIELDS

6. "CD" STANDS FOR:
   A. CORPORATE DECISION
   B. COOL DUDE
   C. COMPACT DISC
   D. COLD DUCK

7. GRACE JONES'S BOYFRIEND IS:

   A. SWEDISH
   B. DANISH
   C. GERMAN
   D. A WOMAN

ROMANTIC EXPERIENCE

8. IT'S ALL RIGHT TO FRENCH KISS ON THE
   1ST 2ND 3RD 4TH 5TH DATE

9. HEAVY PETTING IS ALL RIGHT IF:
   A. YOU ARE IN LOVE, BUT HE'S NOT
   B. HE'S IN LOVE, BUT YOU'RE NOT
   C. YOU'RE BOTH IN LOVE
   D. YOU'RE NOT IN LOVE, BUT YOU KNOW EACH
      OTHER AND YOU WANT TO DO IT
   E. YOU ARE BOTH GOING TO DIFFERENT
      SCHOOLS IN THE FALL
   F. HE BOUGHT YOU A BIG DINNER

10. A WOMAN HAS MORE EROGENOUS ZONES:
   A. ABOVE THE WAIST
   B. BELOW IT

11. CONTRACEPTION SHOULD BE:
   A. LEFT UP TO THE MAN, SINCE IT'S USUALLY HIS
      IDEA
   B. UP TO THE WOMAN, SINCE IT'S HER BODY
   C. UP TO BOTH OF YOU TO TALK ABOUT AND
      AGREE UPON

12. IF I CAUGHT MY GIRLFRIEND OR BOYFRIEND
CHEATING ON ME WITH SOMEONE ELSE, I WOULD:
   A. DROP THEM AND NEVER SPEAK TO THEM
      AGAIN

B. GIVE THEM ANOTHER CHANCE, BUT SECRETLY
   GET EVEN BY CHEATING ON THEM
C. BE ANGRY AT FIRST, BUT ULTIMATELY FORGIVE
   THEM AND TRY TO START OVER

Sylvia thought it was ridiculous but took it anyway, to please her roommates. She decided to answer everything as honestly as she could. If JTK didn't lie, then neither would she. What difference could it make anyway?

That evening at supper, the cafeteria was abuzz with scuttlebut about GOR. Word was, his real name was George Oliver Renville. A search through camp records, going back five years, revealed a sixteen-year-old computer whiz by the name, who, rumor said, had been mauled by a bear. Everybody knew someone who said they remembered reading about it. George was so disfigured that he had a nervous breakdown and had to be put in the nearby State Insane Asylum, where he was kept in a straitjacket until he escaped, two weeks ago, by ripping the jacket apart with his claws. Apparently during the mauling, George had been inoculated with some of the bear's radioactive genetic material, and he had actually cloned real bear paws onto his own arms. (This part was Sylvia's contribution to the story.) Now he was loose. This, by the time dinner was over, was widely known to be true. It hardly mattered when Mrs. Letterer, the camp director, gave a speech to the contrary. She *had* to deny it—it was quite commonly known—so as not to cause a panic.

"It's just so stupid I can't even comment on it," Allexis said. They were in their room tabulating the

CCCCPP scores. Sylvia looked over her roommates' shoulders. The "correct" answers were:

1. B
2. False
3. False
4. It was not cool to smoke.
5. G,D,F,H,B,A,C,E and F,D,G,E,C,A,H,B
6. C
7. Danish
8. 1st
9. C
10. A
11. C
12. A was the best answer, but the others were telling, too.

Virginia knocked on the door, around ten. She asked Sylvia if she could talk with her a minute in the lounge.

"You hear anything?" Virginia asked.

"Well," Sylvia said. "Sort of. I heard from JTK, but he's not GOR. That's what he told me."

"You think he's being straight?" the counselor said.

"I know it," Sylvia said. She didn't know why she trusted him, but she did. How could you have instincts, over a computer terminal? Yet she wanted to believe her feelings. "Okay, I don't know it. It's just that he seems like a very sincere person."

"Not a monster with bear claws?"

"I, uh, sort of started that part of it," Sylvia said. "I certainly didn't expect anyone to believe me. If they thought about it a minute, if he had bear claws, how could he type on a computer keyboard?"

"Well," Virginia said. "Some of the younger kids are so scared they're crying and can't get to sleep. It's not a very funny joke to them. Every year there's some sort of scare like this."

"I'm sorry," Sylvia said. "We'll find him."

"I hope so," Virginia said.

Sylvia and her roommates stayed up until eleven-thirty, talking about first GOR, but then school, boys, politics, parents, music, brothers and sisters, what they wanted to do with their lives, everything. The conversation rambled without direction, but without losing any momentum, either, each of the roommates taking turns. Sylvia liked them. Not counting her dog, Betsy, she'd never had the luxury of someone to talk to while falling asleep before.

She opened her eyes with a start, and looked at the digital clock Sandra had brought. It was 12:09. She hurried down to the lounge, where she entered (FGN/DID!). JTK was waiting for her.

FINALLY! I THOUGHT MAYBE GOR HAD GOTTEN YOU.

I FELL ASLEEP.

STOP! SAY NO MORE. GOR KNOWS HOW TO INTERCEPT AND MONITOR. EVERYTHING WE SAY, HE KNOWS.

BUT HOW?

SHUT UP, SYLVIA! EVERYTHING I SAY COMES OUT SCRAMBLED TO HIM, BUT FOR NOW, HE CAN READ EVERYTHING YOU SAY. YES OR NO, OK?

OK.

NOT OKAY--YES OR NO!

YES.

OKAY. FIRST OF ALL, GOR DOESN'T HAVE TO BE SIGNED IN OR EVEN AWAKE TO BE LISTENING RIGHT NOW. HE COULD AUTO-PILOT SOME MONITOR PROGRAM AND SEARCH TOMMORROW FOR (FGN/DID!). THAT STANDS FOR "FIND GOR NOW--DAMSEL IN DISTRESS," BY THE WAY. NEXT TIME, ADD @#+ BEFORE THE FGN/DID, AND I'LL WRITE IN A PASS CODE SO HE CAN'T MONITOR YOU ANYMORE, EITHER.

THERE'S ONLY ONE M IN TOMORROW.

YEAH YEAH. ALSO, HE DOESN'T EVEN HAVE TO BE IN CAMP. HE COULD BE 3000 MILES AWAY, ACCESSING BY PHONE. THEN AGAIN, WHO'D WANT TO RUN UP A HUGE PHONE BILL, JUST TO SCARE SOME LITTLE KIDS IN A CAMP?

WHO INDEED.

YES OR NO. I RAN THE CAMP RECORDS. THERE REALLY WAS A GEORGE O. RENVILLE, BUT ON THE OTHER HAND, IF I COULD HAVE FOUND THAT OUT, SO COULD GOR. FRANKLY, I'M A LITTLE WORRIED, BECAUSE HE KNOWS YOU AND I ARE AFTER HIM. HE CAN'T GET ME, BUT HE KNOWS WHO YOU ARE. REMEMBER, HE HAS ACCESS TO EVERYTHING YOU'VE ENTERED SO FAR.

SO?

WELL, OKAY. DO YOU HAVE ANY IDEA WHERE THE RUMOR ABOUT GOR BEING A LUNATIC FROM AN INSANE ASYLUM WITH BEAR PAWS INSTEAD OF HANDS CAME FROM?

I ADDED THE PART ABOUT THE PAWS FOR HANDS.

SYLVIA, YES OR NO. PERSONALLY, THAT MAY BE

TRUE, BUT I THINK GOR STARTED THE REST, ABOUT THE BEAR AND THE INSANE ASYLUM. CAN YOU THINK WHERE HE MIGHT HAVE GOTTEN THE IDEA?

   NO.

   YOU MEAN IT DIDN'T RING A BELL WHEN YOU HEARD IT?

   NO.

   I'M SORRY, BUT I'M PRETTY SURE HE GOT IT FROM YOU.

   ?

   I DIDN'T MEAN TO, HONEST, BUT LAST NIGHT WHEN YOU WERE WRITING IN YOUR DIARY, I READ IT.

   NO!

   IT WAS AN . . .

   NO NO NO NO NO NO NO NO NO NO NO NO NO NO NO NO NO NO NO NO NO!!!

   I DIDN'T MEAN . . .

Sylvia logged off and ran back to her room. Reading someone else's diary was about as severe a violation of privacy as anything she could think of—she felt like she'd caught a Peeping Tom in the tree outside her bathroom window. The worst part was how helpless she felt. She was furious and unable to vent it, unable to even find out who to vent it at.

"What's wrong, Syl?" Sandra whispered.

"Nothing," Sylvia said.

On Friday, Virginia announced that the campers were to begin their projects, to be completed by Parents' Day. Sylvia's father said he'd make it if he could. Her project, the program she wanted to write, was something she'd gotten the idea for that spring in school, a short story in which the reader could choose what he or she wanted to have happen to the characters—actually, a parody of romance novels. She hardly felt like writing it anymore.

The first order of business, Virginia said, was for everyone to word-process a description of what they were going to do and then learn how the laser printer worked. It took about an hour for everyone to finish. When they were done, Virginia took everybody over to the Varian and demonstrated the print command routine. With amazing speed the printer generated a separate packet for each student, which Virginia passed out, supposedly containing the project descriptions. The title page of each packet was correct, but on the second page were the now-familiar GOR skull and the words, GOR RULES--COMPLIMENTS OF GOR PUBLICATIONS. Inside the packets were printouts of all the CCCCPPs, with the full name of each girl or boy whose test it was written at the top.

No one could figure out how whoever had printed out the tests for public distribution had been able to match the test to the person who took it, but Sylvia had to admit that the answers on the test with her name on it were her answers. Or she could admit that to herself. In public everybody pretended the names had gotten mixed up. Even so, the embarrassment that spread through the camp was profound.

That day at lunch, Mrs. Letterer delivered an angry lecture on computer etiquette, ethics and abuse. Sylvia and her roommates were called in to Mrs. Letterer's office for the purpose of clarification. Sylvia defended JTK only to the extent that she said she still believed he wasn't GOR. Mrs. Letterer said the scandal was done, and there was no way to put the toothpaste back in the tube. There was nothing to do except carry on. She said a call to the local police department would be in order, if this continued.

In afternoon lab Sylvia logged on to begin her project. She liked, in spite of herself, to read romances. She knew they were nothing like good literature, but then, it didn't say anywhere in the Constitution that people in America are required to have only high aspirations twenty-four hours a day. The right to the pursuit of happiness covered a lot of territory. Sometimes a person needs a little trash in her life, a half hour of watching *The Flintstones* on TV, a Twinkie between meals or maybe a strong dose of loud rock-and-roll once in a while—it does you good. It makes you appreciate the finer things, she'd always thought. The problem with romances was that they always turned out the same, beautiful woman, humble origins, marries wrong, works scrubbing floors in a dungeonlike factory for a mean overseer, enter dark stranger who sweeps her off her feet. All that was nice enough, if that was what you wanted, but sometimes Sylvia wanted things to work out differently.

HELLO, SYLVIA--HOW WAS YOUR LUNCH?

FINE, CECIL. NEW FILE: TITLE: CHOOSE ONE OF THREE.

LOVE'S	DARK	PASSION
PASSION'S	TENDER	DESIRE
DESIRE'S	SACRED	YEARNING
SOUL'S	FLAMING	ACHE

CHAPTER ONE.

JULIA WINTHROP SAT BEFORE THE FIREPLACE, SIPPING A.) SHERRY; B.) BRANDY; C.) CHAMPAGNE; D.) BEER, THINKING OF HOW VERY FAR SHE'D COME IN HER BRIEF A.) 20; B.) 24; C.) 28; D.) 35 YEARS. SHE A.) SIGHED; B.) WEPT SOFTLY; C.) YAWNED; D.) BELCHED. HER HUSBAND, A.) ARMAND; B.) JONATHAN; C.) LORD ALBATTEN; D.) FRANKIE, WAS IN THE OTHER ROOM, DEVOTING ALL HIS CONCENTRATION TO A.) PLAYING HIS VIOLIN; B.) READING; C.) PEELING A BANANA.

Sylvia liked it already. She was about to show Jodie, two terminals down from her, when a skull the size of a dime blinked onto her screen. By now, she thought, it shouldn't surprise her, but it did.

WHAT DO YOU WANT?

The skull smiled an evil smile.

I'M CALLING VIRGINIA, Sylvia entered, but before she had a chance the skull turned sideways, opened its mouth and like Pac-Man gone berserk, began eating Sylvia's sentences. Sylvia screamed for it to stop and hit the escape key, to no effect.

"Virginia," she shouted, "GOR's on my screen!" Five seconds later, the whole class was looking over Sylvia's shoulder. The skull paused from devouring Sylvia's words at BRIEF.

HA HA HA--GOR RULES! YOU'LL NEVER CATCH ME!

"Oh wow," Sandra said.

The skull laughed again in defiance, electronically cruel, mathematically inscrutable. Sylvia could only watch. The skull stopped a moment to enjoy his advantage. Then suddenly, from nowhere, a spaceship appeared, similar to an Asteroids ship but sleeker, more elegant and slightly larger. It locked onto the skull and fired four photon torpedos, blowing it clear out of the sky.

"What was that?" a boy said.

DUT-DADA-DUH! JTK RULES! COME AND GET ME GOR, YOU SLIMY PIG.

"Oh, Sylvia," Jodie said, "un-beee-lievable."

A second skull appeared, using what remained of Sylvia's project as a barricade. JTK's ship stopped firing and began to circle slowly up the left side of the monitor, facing GOR, who retreated down the right side. When they were opposite each other, the skull disappeared off the right side of the screen and reappeared on the left, behind the ship, eating it.

A new ship appeared. JTK and GOR resumed their game of cat and mouse. GOR tried the cross-screen wraparound a second time but JTK hit hyperspace and escaped. The onlookers oohed. JTK began to chase GOR around the paragraph, faster and faster, firing occasional chaser shots—then suddenly, the ship reversed direction and fired a shot, on the glide, with uncanny accuracy down the channel between the first and second line of Sylvia's story, catching GOR square in the ear, blowing him away.

YOU WIN THIS TIME, JTK. WE WILL MEET AGAIN.

ANYTIME, SLIMEBALL.

After supper, without twenty people looking over her shoulder, Sylvia logged on with (@#+FGN/DID!) and waited, summoning JTK like a genie from a magic lantern. He was waiting for her call.

MY HERO.

SHUCKS.

YOU'RE LUCKY I'M TALKING TO YOU AT ALL.

I KNOW.

I'M STILL MAD AT YOU--DON'T YOU EVER READ MY DIARY AGAIN. DO YOU UNDERSTAND?

YES. I'M SORRY. I SAID I WAS SORRY. IT WAS AN ACCIDENT. I WAS JUST TRYING TO WARN YOU THAT IF I COULD DO IT, GOR COULD, TOO, AND PROBABLY HAS ALREADY.

WE HAVE TO FIND THAT *&(%*%#%$@! I NEED YOUR HELP. WILL YOU TEACH ME WHAT YOU KNOW?

MAYBE. SOMEDAY. IT'S COMPLICATED.

I'M SMART.

I KNOW.

HOW DID YOU DO ALL THAT, THIS AFTER-NOON? WHAT KIND OF COMPUTER ARE YOU USING?

SAME ONE YOU ARE. HOW ELSE COULD I TALK TO YOU?

BE COY, WHY DON'T YOU? OKAY. SO ANYWAY, WHAT'S THE PLAN?

WELL, IT ISN'T GEORGE RENVILLE. I CHECKED ALL THE RECORDS I COULD GET A BYTE ON AND FOUND OUT HE'S IN SUMMER SCHOOL AT STANFORD. I RAIDED THEIR APOLLO SYSTEM. ANYWAY, WHOEVER IT IS IS PRETTY SHARP, AND HE'S GOT A TON OF PERIPHERY, A MODEM TO CECIL. DEFINITELY SUPER-USER, VIA SOME TRAPDOORS BEHIND HIM, OR SOME SUCH BLIND. THE PASS CODES ARE SOFT, AND THEY CAN'T LEAP THE MAINFRAME WITHOUT THE PHONE COMPANY, ASSUMING HE'S OFF CAMPUS, AND NOT HARD-WIRED. THEY COULD EITHER CHANGE THE SUBS AND ENCRYPT OR WRITE THE PRIMITIVES ON PAPER, BUT THEY'D PROBABLY RATHER HAVE HIM

RIDING IT THAN LOSE HIM ENTIRELY. IF IT WAS ME, I'D DITCH HIM BEFORE HE TIME-BOMBS THE KERNELS. THEY MUST WANT TO TALK TO HIM.

TRY THAT AGAIN IN ENGLISH.

IN ENGLISH, HE WROTE A SECRET WAY BACK INTO THE CAMPUS MAINFRAME, SO THAT THEY CAN'T EXCLUDE HIM, ONCE THEY CHANGE THE CODES, AND IT'S BLIND, MEANING THEY CAN'T SEARCH FOR ANOMALIES TO LOCATE THE TRAPDOOR. THE MAIN-FRAME IS WIRED TO THE CAMPUS SWITCHBOARD FOR STUDENT AND FACULTY USE, NOT A WIDE-ACCESS COMPUTER THAT THE SCHOOL BUYS TIME ON THEY COULD CHANGE THE SUBPROGRAMS AND ENCRYPT THEM AND THEN KEEP TRACK OF WHAT THEY'VE DONE ON PAPER, NOT IN THE COMPUTER, WHERE GOR COULD FIND IT, TOO, MAYBE, BUT RATH-ER THAN LOSE HIM, THEY WANT TO KEEP HIM ON LINE, LIKE KEEPING A KIDNAPPER ON THE PHONE, SO THEY CAN MORE OR LESS TRACE THE CALL AND FIND HIM, BUT THEY'RE TAKING THE RISK AND BET-TING THAT GOR ISN'T SMART ENOUGH TO TIME-BOMB THE CORE DATA IN THE WHOLE SYSTEM, MEANING TO WRITE A BLIND PROGRAM THAT DIRECTS CECIL TO ERASE EVERYTHING IN HIM AT A GIVEN TIME IN THE FUTURE, AFTER GOR HAS DISAPPEARED AND GONE BACK TO WHEREVER HE CAME FROM. IT'S A DEVICE USED BY DISGRUNTLED PROGRAMMERS WHO GET FIRED FROM COMPANIES AND WANT TO SEEK RE-VENGE BY BRINGING THE PEOPLE WHO FIRED THEM TO FINANCIAL RUIN SOMETIMES THEY JUST INSTALL A SIEVE AND DRAIN CORPORATE FUNDS. THERE'S ALL KINDS OF FUN THINGS YOU CAN DO IF YOU KNOW HOW.

I GUESS THERE ARE.

IT DOESN'T MATTER. ANYWAY, THE PLAN I HAVE IS THIS. I'LL CHALLENGE GOR TO A DUEL, AT SOME SORT OF STUPID VIDEO GAME, AS YOU PUT IT, AND I'M SURE HE'LL TAKE ME UP ON IT, SINCE I BET HE'S REAL COCKY, AND THEN I'LL WRITE A KILL PROGRAM INTO THE CHALLENGE, SO THAT WHICHEVER OF US LOSES THE GAME WILL HAVE EVERYTHING IN HIS COMPUTER ERASED FOREVER. TOTAL ANNIHILATION. IF I BEAT HIM IT WILL COST HIM MONEY AND MORE IMPORTANT, TIME TO RECOMPILE, AND WHEN HE DOES THAT THERE WILL PROBABLY BE DATA BASES HE'LL NEED THAT WE CAN WATCH, MAYBE FIND HIM THAT WAY.

DON'T.

WHY NOT?

WHAT IF YOU LOSE?

HOW CAN I LOSE?

I THINK I LIKE YOU. WHOEVER YOU ARE.

YOU DO?

YES. YOU'RE A GOOD GUY.

I LIKE YOU, TOO. DON'T WORRY. EVERYTHING WILL BE OKAY.

That night, the counselors were going to take the campers out on the lake in boats, for a lecture on the constellations. When Phil turned the light on at the college boathouse, one camper noticed a sign on the door, a piece of paper with a skull drawn in Magic Marker and the words, "GOR WARNS YOU. DEATH TO CAMPERS. ESPECIALLY YOU, SYLVIA!"

Over half the campers wanted to go back. Everyone

gathered in the dorm commons room, hoping there would be security in numbers, boys and girls alike, listening to records. Some played chess, or monopoly. Rumors circulated. Men from the Insane Asylum supposedly had the whole campus staked out. A cow on a nearby farm was said to have been found slashed to death by what appeared to be bear claws. Shapes were seen in the shadows beyond the windows and in the woods.

DAY THIRTEEN

DEAR DIARY,

HOW APPROPRIATELY SUPERSTITIOUS. RECEIVED MY FIRST DEATH THREAT TODAY FROM MY GOOD FRIEND GOR. HE'S SO COOL, AND SMART AND WONDERFUL--I DON'T KNOW HOW HE DOES IT. SERIOUSLY, HE HATES ME, BUT I DON'T HATE HIM. I DON'T KNOW WHY HE DOESN'T LIKE ME. I REALLY WANT TO MEET HIM. I DON'T CARE ANYMORE IF HE DOES KNOW HOW TO READ MY DIARY. IF YOU'RE READING THIS, GOR, JUST TELL ME WHERE YOU WANT TO RENDEZVOUS, AND I'LL BE THERE. I HAVE A VERY SEXY DRESS I BROUGHT WITH ME THAT I'D LOVE TO SHOW YOU. I'D LOVE TO WALK UP TO YOU AND SMILE SHYLY AT YOU, BECAUSE I REALLY AM SHY, AND LICK MY LIPS AS I GOT CLOSER AND CLOSER TO YOU, AND THEN WHEN I GOT RIGHT UP TO YOU, I'D PUT MY ARMS AROUND YOU AND CLOSE MY EYES AND LEAN MY HEAD FORWARD PUCKERING MY LIPS UNTIL MY MOUTH IS RIGHT NEXT TO

YOUR EAR AND THEN WITHOUT WARNING I
WOULD PUT MY KNEE IN THAT LAST PLACE
YOU'D EVER WANT IT AND TURN YOU DEEP
GREEN WITH NAUSEA AND MAKE YOU MORE
OF A SOPRANO THAN YOU ALREADY ARE,
YOU OBNOXIOUS LITTLE PIECE OF DUNG.

Sylvia missed the second call to breakfast the next
morning, after which she hurried down to the cafeteria, where she found her roommates finishing their
meals. When she sat down next to Allexis, all three,
without a word, rose and moved to another table.
Sylvia thought it was a joke. She felt like everybody
was staring at her. She got up to join her friends.

"Stay where you are!" Allexis said.

"If you don't want to eat with us, we don't want to
eat with you," Sandra said, adding, "like!"

"What's the matter with you?" Sylvia said.

"Nothing's the matter with us," Jodie said. She
threw a piece of paper at Sylvia. "This was slipped
under all the doors this morning." Sylvia read it, a
computer printout, headed, COMPLIMENTS OF GOR
PUBLICATIONS. It read:

DAY THREE

DEAR DIARY,

A BOY LIKES ME. I SWOON. I SWOON. I NOW
HAVE A SECRET ADMIRER WHO HAS FOUND A
WAY TO CRASH MY PROGRAM AND LEAVE MESSAGES. I SAY TO MYSELF, WHY NOT? WHAT'S THE
BIG DEAL. BE HONEST WITH YOURSELF.

THE ROOMMATE SITUATION: SANDRA SAYS
"LIKE" TOO MUCH (LIKE, ALL THE, LIKE, TIME),

JODIE IS OVERWEIGHT AND WEARS TOO MUCH
MAKEUP, AND ALLEXIS IS AN ANOREXIC J.A.P.
SNOB. I WANT MY MONEY BACK.

Twenty minutes later, all four girls were in Mrs.
Letterer's office, for the second time in as many days.
Sylvia, upset as she was, could nevertheless under-
stand how her roommates must feel.

"That's not what I wrote," she said.

"Did GOR write this then?" Mrs. Letterer asked.

"Well, no," Sylvia said, "I did, but there was more.
He changed it." She handed Mrs. Letterer her diary.
When the camp director put it up on the screen, what
Sylvia had written the night before was there, but
what she had written the night of the third day was
missing.

"GOR erased my diary," Sylvia said, "I don't
believe it."

"That's possible," Virginia said, "I found it in the
drive on a terminal in the third-floor lounge the next
morning. He could have copied it and erased the
original."

"So what?" Sandra said. "She still wrote what we
read."

Sylvia reasserted that there was more and said she
could prove it.

(@#+FGN/DID!) JTK--DAMSEL IN DISTRESS!
URGENT!

"JTK was reading my diary that night, too," Sylvia
said. "Sandra, remember when I came in and you
said, 'what's wrong?' and I said it was nothing? That
was when. He'll tell you." She waited a full minute.

JTK--WHERE ARE YOU? DAMSEL IN DISTRESS!

Another minute passed.

"Really, you guys. He's not there now, but . . ."

YOU RANG? SORRY. I WAS IN THE BATHROOM. EVEN SAVIORS OF THE UNIVERSE HAVE TO PEE ONCE IN A WHILE.

WATCH YOUR MOUTH, STUPID. MRS. LETTER-ER IS STANDING RIGHT BEHIND ME.

OH. I BEG YOUR PARDON, MADAM.

First Allexis asked JTK what Sylvia had said about her, then Sandra and Jodie. In each case, JTK was able to recall word for word the nice things Sylvia had said. Sandra admitted that her parents were always correcting her language. Jodie said maybe she could lose ten pounds. Allexis said she'd always known she was a snob. The four roommates hugged each other and said what they'd do to GOR when they caught him. JTK said in parting to start spreading the word:

TOMORROW NIGHT. 10:00. DUEL TO THE DEATH. GOR CAN NAME THE GAME. LOSER GETS GHOSTED.

The tension mounted all the next day. GOR left a message on every terminal: JTK DIES TONIGHT--GOR RULES THE K! WITNESS THE SLAUGHTER! Kids made signs and banners. Predictably, some of the boys on the fourth floor, the dungeon-heads with the heavy-metal T-shirts, came out supporting GOR, drawing skulls on their sweatshirts with Magic Markers. An Advent screen projector television was set up in the commons, for the whole camp to watch. Virginia told Sylvia, in confidence, that if everyone in camp attended, heads could be counted, and whoever wasn't there would have to be either JTK or GOR. Sylvia wasn't so sure. She thought she'd started to have the first inkling of a better idea.

By late afternoon it had clouded over. By eight it was raining, complete with lightning and thunder. Perfect weather. By nine-thirty the commons room was packed and raucous. On the wall to either side of the television screen hung bed sheets, with GOR and a skull on one, JTK and his ship on the other. Everybody was chanting. Sylvia was alone in the lounge, at the terminal.

WE'RE ALL SET JTK. HOW DO YOU FEEL?

I FEEL GREAT. HOW DO YOU FEEL?

I CAN'T WAIT TO GET MY HANDS ON THIS TWERP. BUT I'M A LITTLE NERVOUS TOO.

THAT'S NORMAL.

ARE YOU?

NO.

MACHO DUDE PLUS GALORE. LISTEN, I HAD AN IDEA. IF GOR ERASED MY FLOPPY DISK DIARY, THEN HE HAD TO HAVE SNUCK INTO THE LOUNGE AND TAKEN IT OUT OF THE SLOT OR USED THE TERMINAL RIGHT THERE, BECAUSE I TURNED THE MACHINE OFF WHEN I WAS DONE, AND HE COULDN'T HAVE TURNED IT BACK ON FROM REMOTE, RIGHT? YOU HAVE TO DO THAT PHYSI-CALLY, RIGHT?

RIGHT. SO?

SO HE HAS TO BE ON CAMPUS, NOT OFF.

GOOD. AND?

AND, THEN, HE HAS TO USE A CAMPUS PHONE TO GET INTO CECIL, AND UNLESS I'M MISTAKEN, I'LL BET YOU ANYTHING THERE'S A CAMPUS

PHONE SYSTEM WHERE ANY PHONE IN USE WILL LIGHT UP AT THE SWITCHBOARD. SO ALL WE HAVE TO DO IS HAVE SOMEONE STAND BY THE SWITCHBOARD, WATCH WHAT LIGHTS LIGHT AND GO THERE WHILE YOU'RE DUELING.

GREAT IDEA. UNLESS A LOT OF PEOPLE ARE USING THE PHONES.

DOUBTFUL--IT'S THE MIDDLE OF SUMMER, LATE AT NIGHT, AND THE COMPUTER CAMP IS THE ONLY GROUP USING THE CAMPUS AT THE MOMENT.

I SEE.

SO JUST TELL ME WHICH PHONE YOU'LL BE USING, SO WE CAN GO TO THE OTHER ONE AND TRACK GOR DOWN.

I CAN'T DO THAT, OR YOU'LL BE ABLE TO FIND ME, TOO.

JTK! YOU WIENER, DON'T YOU WANT TO MEET ME IN PERSON?

SURE. BUT NOT NOW. NOT YET, ANYWAY.

LOOK, I NEED TO KNOW, SO WE CAN FIND GOR.

DON'T WORRY ABOUT IT. I WON'T USE A CAMPUS PHONE.

YOU'RE NOT ON CAMPUS?

I DIDN'T SAY THAT. I CAN'T TELL YOU. JUST TRUST ME.

BUT WHAT IF YOU LOSE? HOW WILL WE GET BACK IN TOUCH?

HOW CAN I LOSE?

WHAT IF I NEVER SEE YOU AGAIN?

WHAT DO YOU MEAN, AGAIN? YOU HAVEN'T SEEN ME YET.

I KNOW. WHY?

WOULDN'T YOU LIKE TO KNOW.

WHY NOT JUST COME UP AND SAY HELLO?

I'M SHY I'M SHY I'M SHY I'M SHY I'M SHY I'M SHY I'M SHY I'M SHY!

ARE YOU SHY?

YES.

WHY?

WOULDN'T I LIKE TO KNOW. I JUST AM. YOU'RE THE FIRST GIRL I EVER EVEN TOLD. I'VE NEVER EVEN KISSED A GIRL.

WHAT A BOZO. IT'S OK. I SHOULD GO. IT'S ALMOST TIME. YOU READY?

RARING.

I LIKE YOU. IT'S EASIER SOMEHOW, MEETING LIKE THIS. ALL I KNOW ABOUT YOU IS WHAT YOU TELL ME--IT'S ALMOST LIKE MEETING AT A MAS-QUERADE PARTY, WHERE YOU REALLY CAN'T TELL WHO THE OTHER PERSON IS. I LIKE IT, BUT STILL, I THINK WE SHOULD GET TOGETHER. WIN OR LOSE, WILL YOU MEET ME TOMORROW AT THE SPOT WHERE THE CAMPFIRE WAS? THREE O'CLOCK?

MAYBE.

YES OR NO!

YES.

At five minutes to ten, the lights in the commons room were turned off, and the television was on. Sylvia was stationed in the commons room kitchen, where she could see the screen and still answer the phone. Allexis was at the student union, near the campus switchboard. Sylvia had asked the operator, when she was on duty earlier in the day, for a list of which exchanges were where in which dorms or campus buildings. Allexis would call Sylvia as soon as a line lit up. Sandra and Jodie were in the crowd, looking for anything suspicious. Virginia was by the door, near Sylvia.

At ten o'clock the red, white and blue image of a waving American flag appeared on the screen, and an electronic version of the Star Spangled Banner was heard. Incredibly corny, Sylvia thought. She was liking this guy more and more. The campers sang along at the top of their voices.

THIS PATRIOTIC MESSAGE BROUGHT TO YOU BY JTK.

Somebody yelled, "Play ball!"

I'M READY, GOR, YOU DONKEY-BREATHED NERD. LET'S GO.

A skull appeared after the word "go" and ate JTK's challenge, Pac-Manlike.

SCARE ME, GOR. LAST TIME I SAW THAT PROGRAM, IT WAS SO FUNNY I FORGOT TO FALL OFF MY DINO-SAUR.

YOU DIE, ROCKETMAN!

The field switched to a maze of green lines, viewed from above, human stick figures in opposite corners, GOR in red, JTK in blue. Virginia whispered to Sylvia that it looked like a form of Berserk, though unless she missed her guess, it wouldn't surprise her to see GOR rewriting professional, copyrighted programs. Each character had a gun in his hand. The idea was to work your way through the maze, shooting at your opponent through windows and gaps. The duelists began to move, JTK firing through windows, his bullets bouncing off the walls, ricocheting, GOR holding fire. JTK stopped, positioning himself at a window. GOR raised his gun at the motionless JTK. JTK moved. Where JTK's bullets bounced off the walls of the maze, GOR's went right through them.

"Unfair," someone yelled.

"JTK doesn't have a chance," someone else said, and everybody seemed to agree. Nobody, however, told JTK.

He moved like a frenetic bumblebee, feinting, altering speeds, up, back, left, right. GOR fired shot after shot through the walls. JTK was a lightning quick bantamweight, ducking in and out of the slow heavyweight's punches, bobbing, weaving. Sylvia wanted the phone to ring.

Gradually JTK drew nearer and nearer his opponent, ducking, dipping, dancing between bullets, dodging, slip-sliding, never a false step, until he was so close GOR's shots missed by mere millimeters. Soon it was GOR who was in danger. GOR backed down a corridor, firing as he moved, unable to draw a bead, until he was forced to run. JTK rushed him. GOR couldn't shoot and run at the same time, panicked, fleeing blindly, JTK in hot pursuit. The crowd roared. GOR had run into a corner, JTK right on top of him, skipping, shuffling, in out. GOR was going to lose, so GOR switched games. Suddenly the maze was replaced with a simulated race track.

"Coward," the cry went up. There was a chorus of boos.

"It's Indy—I've played this," somebody next to Sylvia said. It was Phil, who'd joined Virginia at the door. GOR's candy-apple-red racer idled a quarter mile up the track from JTK. The game would be over when one of them crashed, either into an outside wall, an inside post, one of the slower cars or each other. The campers heard JTK shift into first, getting a feel for the road, doing a mere eighty, according to the speedometer, superimposed in the lower right-hand corner. GOR's speedometer, lower left, also read eighty. JTK swerved to avoid a pothole.

"A pothole?" Phil said to Virginia. "There aren't any potholes in this game." A second pothole loomed ahead, a stalled car blocking the path around it. JTK sped up and jumped it.

"That's not, either, I'll bet," Virginia said.

"A jump function?" Phil said. "Amazing. These guys are rewriting left and right. I couldn't do that one."

JTK's speedometer climbed, as did GOR's, the two cars snaking in and out of traffic at 180 mph. JTK was a few feet off GOR's tail and drafting, when an oil slick spilled from the back of the red car. JTK jumped the slick but fell back. GOR's bag of dirty tricks seemed bottomless. GOR pulled ahead, and for several laps, the dotted white line was a blur. JTK navigated deftly around hazards GOR put in his path.

Then GOR's speedometer dropped to 150, his red car stalled behind two slower cars driving side by side. JTK's speedometer jumped to 240. GOR spread out a long, defensive oil slick behind him. JTK was doing 285 when he hit the edge of the slick and jumped, flying through the air. In another second, his blue car would land directly on top of GOR's, annihilating them both.

GOR switched games again.

"Battlezone," Phil said. The visual of Indianapolis

Speedway was gone, in its place, an eerie, otherworldly black landscape, green lines describing geometric cubes, pyramids and pillboxes dotting the terrain, a green-lined volcano spouting green lava in the distance. The sound of whining high-performance race car engines gave way to the low rumbling of tanks. In the video-parlor version, the object was to score points with your tank by shooting enemy tanks, missiles, saucers and supertanks, using the geometric bulletproof forms to hide behind. Phil said he'd never seen the game played head to head, though he knew the army had an advanced tank training program.

"It couldn't be," he said. "If it is, these guys know ADA. That's a Defense Department language. That is serious crime hacking. We're talking national security violations."

A blip on the radar screen showed something just over the horizon. JTK's tank growled slowly forward to meet the fray. A glowing shell came streaking out of the night toward JTK, who quickly reversed direction; the shell flew harmlessly over him. GOR had given his position away. JTK retreated, taking refuge behind a pyramid. The room hushed.

"He's testing him," Phil said. "He wants to see if GOR can shoot through obstacles, the way he shot through the walls in the maze." GOR's tank loomed at the edge of vision, a muzzle flash signaling that another shell was on its way. GOR's shot hit the pyramid and detonated.

"A fair fight?" Virginia said. "That's not like GOR."

A missile zigzagged out of the sky at JTK, who picked it off before it reached him.

"You're premature," Phil said. "Some fair fight. JTK's got to play the drones *and* contend with GOR at the same time."

JTK fought in reverse gear, nailing missiles, tanks and saucers, usually with his first shot, while at the same time avoiding GOR's salvos. Fighting while driving in reverse had the added risk of backing into unseen objects—and once you stopped moving, your coordinates fixed, you were dead. Yet JTK seemed to have the territory memorized. Sylvia noticed, as JTK held his own, that a change had occurred. Nobody was rooting for GOR anymore.

The phone rang.

"Allexis?"

"Well of course it's Allexis, dodo—who else would it be? Listen—*the phone is somewhere in the dorm.* But the deal is, something got rewired or something, because *all* the exchanges are lit."

"Here? In this building?"

"That's what the switchboard says. How's it going?"

"I'll tell you later," Sylvia said, slamming the phone down on the hook. She found Sandra and Jodie. The student phones were in the lounges. Sandra was to search the boys' wing, Jodie the girls'. If they found anybody they'd rendezvous back in the kitchen and make the capture together.

JTK was stopped behind a cube, GOR behind another cube about a kilometer away. GOR hoped the drones would distract JTK enough to give him an easy shot, but JTK was just too good. GOR nosed out from behind his cube and began to run toward the volcano. For the first time JTK moved full speed.

"GOR doesn't have to run," Phil said. "This could be a setup."

In real Battlezone, Phil said, the mountain images in the distance are unapproachable, neither growing in size as you drive toward them nor shrinking as you back away. GOR had changed that. After several seconds of chase the flat landscape gave way to rolling foothills. Occasionally JTK would get a shot off, only to see GOR's tank duck down the back slope of a hill.

The pursuit wound up a twisting mountain road, the back of GOR's tank peeking into view every so often, rounding a curve. The terrain dropped sharply away from the road, and the slightest mistake meant a thousand-foot tumble.

The road opened onto a flat plateau, a box canyon, at the end of which was a sheer rock face. GOR was headed for a tunnel at the base. JTK locked him in his sights and fired, but GOR was too far ahead, and the volley fell short. GOR disappeared into the mountain. Obviously he wanted JTK to follow him. JTK stopped, out of range of the tunnel. Jodie burst through the door, panting.

"He's not in the girls' wing," she said. "What's happening?"

"GOR's in the tunnel," Sylvia said. Sandra came in, equally out of breath.

"Zero," she said.

"Just what are you girls up to?" Virginia asked.

"Virginia," Sylvia said, "how many phones are there in the dorm?"

"Well," she said, "eight lounges, this one, in the kitchen, the front desk, and the Head Resident's apartment, but she's gone. Why?"

Sylvia could see the front desk from where she stood. There was no one there.

"It's got to be the Head Resident's apartment," Sylvia said. "GOR's broken into it." Sylvia explained everything to Virginia. Virginia said she'd check it out with Phil.

Meanwhile, JTK had decided to press the issue, again, bobbing, ducking, weaving, all of GOR's shots missing. The excitement was almost unbearable as JTK approached the mouth of the cave. GOR was somewhere inside the mountain, location unknown, radar inoperable. JTK waited outside the mouth for one last shot from GOR, then dove into the pitchblack void.

"Nothing," Phil said, returning with Virginia. "He must not be in the dorm. Where are the tanks?"

"But he has to be," Sylvia said. "They're inside the volcano." Visible now, only the muzzle flashes, and ghostly vectors left by the streaking green projectiles in the darkness. JTK held his fire, navigating only by sound. GOR seemed somewhere off to the left. JTK rumbled forward at half throttle.

There was a sudden bonk! JTK had collided with something. He fired. Nothing. He pulled back—a muzzle flashed not two feet in front of him, missing. He reversed, turned, fired, nothing, drew back, arced left, fired, nothing, and retreated. He'd run smack into GOR and lost him.

"I gotta eat something," Jodie said. "This is too much."

GOR's engine was distant, getting fainter. He was running again. At the top of the screen, slightly to the left, a dot of light appeared, an exit from the cave. The question was, what was on the other side? JTK stopped.

"He'll blast GOR when he tries to get out," Jodie said.

"He'll have to lead him from this distance," Phil said. "If he misses, he'll be a sitting duck when it's his turn to leave." JTK fired. GOR scurried through the opening. JTK missed.

JTK's engines roared to life, angry, determined, caution thrown to the proverbial wind.

"Don't be foolish, JTK," Sylvia heard herself say. The onlookers picked up the chant again, "JTK, JTK, JTK . . ."

He burst through the cave's exit to find himself on the streets of Aspen, Colorado.

"What?" Sandra asked.

"Oh wow," Phil said, "Unbelievable. Aspen—I've heard about this. Some guy took movies of every possible street and direction in Aspen, Colorado, from every angle, and put it all on a disk. In the real game, you maneuver through the streets. But with two tanks? Amazing."

Radar said GOR was up ahead. A light snow was falling as JTK rolled his tank into the peaceful little skiing village. It was like being part of a movie. Passersby with skis over their shoulders looked on with surprise. At an intersection, JTK stopped, looked right, then left, for GOR.

"What's the matter with him?" Virginia said. "Radar says GOR's up ahead at eleven o'clock."

"Maybe the blip's a decoy," Phil said.

"Maybe he's just pretending he can't see it," Sylvia said.

JTK turned off Main Street in front of a clothing store and down a side road. GOR was three blocks north, moving parallel.

"I'll bet he's jamming JTK's radar," Phil said.

JTK looked up a side street toward GOR, but GOR stopped just short of the intersection, out of sight. JTK continued, going straight. GOR turned south, then east. He was right behind JTK, but apparently JTK didn't know it.

JTK stopped at an alley. GOR, not ten feet behind him, waited, enjoying his cloak of invisibility. JTK turned up the alley.

"Oh no," a boy up front yelled. "I played this before. That alley's a dead end."

The crowd fell silent. JTK drove slowly, looking into each garage, oblivious to GOR, thirty feet behind him, doomed.

"Last game, too," Phil said. "There's no other game for GOR to switch to on video disk."

JTK reached the end of the alley. GOR stopped, forty feet behind, the alley too narrow for JTK to turn around in.

"Goodbye, JTK," Sandra said, "you did good."

JTK's tank began to move in reverse. GOR waited. JTK was ten feet away, point-blank range. GOR fired.

JTK hit the jump button and sailed clear over GOR.

"He jumped!" Phil shouted. "I completely forgot."

The crowd was delirious, chanting JTK! JTK! JTK!, for it was GOR, now, who was trapped. JTK drove forward, bumping GOR, gunned his thundering engines, bulldozing him forward, GOR spinning his treads helplessly in reverse, until JTK had GOR pinned against the brick wall of a warehouse.

GIVE UP, GOR?

GOR RULES THE . . .

OH SHUT UP!

JTK fired a single blast, which shattered GOR's tank into a dozen pieces, spinning out into space. Two hundred and six campers, minus GOR and JTK, of course, exploded in unbridled ovation. Popcorn flew through the air, toilet paper streamers, sofa cushions, camp beanies. The boys in GOR T-shirts took them off and tore them into shreds. Sylvia, Sandra and Jodie hugged each other, jumping up and down.

DUT-DADA-DAH!!! JTK, SAVIOR OF THE UNIVERSE, THANKS YOU.

"Wait a minute," Sylvia said.

"What?" Jodie asked.

"Wait a doggone minute. Virginia, is it just a regular phone at the front desk, or is it a kind of miniswitchboard with buttons on it, that all the lines in the dorm run through?"

"It's a miniswitchboard," Virginia said.

"Right," Sylvia said, "so during school, someone sits there and answers the phone so that they don't ring in the halls during study hours, right?"

"She buzzes whoever has a call," Virginia said.

"I knew it!" Sylvia said. "It has to be the front desk. Come on."

A colossal oak desk, ten feet long and four feet deep, sat in a glassed-in office by the door. Sylvia, Sandra, Jodie and Allexis tiptoed up to it as quietly as they could.

"Where's the telephone?" Allexis whispered. "It's not on the desk. Shouldn't there be one?"

Sylvia put her finger to her lips. She looked behind the desk, and traced the phone wire from the jack to a hole in the back of the desk itself. Sylvia knelt and put her ear to the cupboard door. She could make out a faint whimpering inside.

"Okay you little rat," she said, flinging the door open, "come out or I'll drag you out!"

Crouched inside the desk, before what Phil later said had to be ten thousand dollars' worth of equipment, all brought from home, illuminated by the blue light of his video screen, was a ten-year-old boy with tears running down his face.

"I want my mommy!" he said. "I don't wanna be in camp. I want my mommy! I wanna go home!"

"Who's this?" Virginia said, standing in the doorway.

"Virginia," Sylvia said, "meet GOR."

The next day at five minutes to three, Sylvia was sitting on a log by the fire pit, wearing her sexiest cutoffs and a JTK T-shirt Sandra had given her. Allexis had let her use some of her most expensive perfume. She was staring up the path toward the dorm when someone coughed behind her, a boy, about her age, straddling a bicycle. A bike path led along the shore to the town.

"Hi," he said.

"Hi," she said, perturbed at the intrusion.

"You go to college here?"

"It's a summer camp for people to learn computers," she said. He relaxed his brakes. "You a townie?"

"Yeah," he said. "Computers, huh?"

"Look," she said, "I'm waiting for somebody. Do you mind? It's important."

"It's a free country," the kid said.

"Okay, fine," she said, angry, "just leave, please. What do you want?"

"Wouldn't you like to know?"

"JTK?" Sylvia said, her mouth falling open. The boy smiled. "Where'd you get a bicycle?"

"My dad gave it to me," he said, getting off it. "He bought it at a store."

"Don't be a wise guy—how'd they let you bring a bicycle to camp? No one else has one."

"I'm not in camp," he said, "I really do live in town."

Sylvia didn't know what to say.

"I saw you the second day, when they bused everybody to Shakey's for pizza. I was in the corner, playing Donkey Kong. I thought you were the prettiest girl there, so I pretended I was a camper and asked somebody what your name was."

"But how did you get into the school computer, Cecil?"

"Well, we got a VAX at our house, bigger than Cecil," JTK said. "My dad's a professor, but he also writes software for Wang Laboratories, you know, research and stuff, and makes up games on the side. He's got a line to the college for some of his work. Anyway, he's been testing stuff on me since I was three. I was gonna maybe go to camp, but there's not a lot I could learn. I've been writing my own games and programming since I was seven. Actually, I sold one to Gottleib, but they never developed it."

"You're great," Sylvia said. JTK blushed.

"Well. For a hacker," he said. "My dad's in Germany at a conference. He said I could do whatever I wanted to. You find GOR, by the way?"

"He turned out to be a little rich kid, one of the special child prodigy students they brought in. He's only ten, but in computer age, he's up to the level of a junior in high school. I was going to punch him out, but when I saw how little he was, I couldn't do it."

"I figured he had dough," JTK said. "Actually, I was sort of toying with him. I haven't lost a video game since I was six, when my dad . . . uh, what are you doing?"

Sylvia walked up to him and put her face a few inches from his.

"You smell great," he said. She took his hands in hers.

"I still don't know your real name," she said.

"Uh, Tom," he said. "Tom Newberry."

"Tom Newberry?" Sylvia said. "What's the JTK for?"

"Actually," Tom said, "it stands for James T. Kirk."

"Who's he?"

"Who's he? You've never seen *Star Trek?*"

"Of course I have," she said.

"Are you going to kiss me?" he said.

"Wouldn't you like to know?" she said. She put her arms around him, closed her eyes and kissed, counting silently.

"Have you really never kissed a girl?" she asked him.

"Now I have," he said.

"But before? Why not?"

"I told you. I'm shy. I know some girls at school. Mostly it's easier to stay home and write programs."

"There's a lot you could teach me," Sylvia said.

"There's a lot you could teach me," Tom Newberry said.

"Let's get started then," Sylvia said.

They kissed again.

"Hey," Sylvia said, laughing, "you're not supposed to do that until the third date."

"Sorry," Tom said. "Once I learn the rules to something, I have a hard time not rewriting them."

"Me too," Sylvia said.

They kissed again.

About the Author

PETE NELSON was born on the South Side of Chicago at the turn of the century with a guitar around his neck and a harmonica in his mouth in a tarpaper shack he built with his bare hands. The son of a barrelhouse piano player and barrel-housekeeper, by the time he was five, Nelson had picked up the sobriquet "Professor," or "'Foss." When he donned a pair of dark glasses at age ten and pretended to be blind, selling pencils on the street outside the Commodities Exchange, he became known as "Blind Professor" Pete Nelson and later "Blind Professor Pork Bellies Pete Nelson" which was shortened to "Blind Belly Nelson." A diminutive lad who never grew much bigger than a weimeraner, in his teens he was known as "Little Blind Belly Pete" and "Little Blind Baby Face Professor Belly Nelson." In 1932, Nelson moved to Mississippi and became known as "Little Blind Mississippi Belly Faced Baby Muddy Professor Pete" or "The Delta Dog." After the big band era arrived, introducing America to musicians with names like "Duke" Ellington and "Count" Basie and Nat "King" Cole, Nelson took on the dub

"Little Blind Mississippi Belly Faced Muddy Professor Delta Dog Pete The-Prince-of-Wales Nelson."

Oddly enough, despite all his nicknames, Nelson is completely tone deaf and has never actually played a note or learned a single blues song, his frequent monickering the result of an accident at birth by which he was born with a guitar around his neck and a harmonica in his mouth (an errant El train had crashed into a music store next door to the tarpaper shack he built with his bare hands). Ironically, the son Nelson fathered while in Tupelo, Elvis Aaron Presley, went on to achieve a degree of musical notoriety, and still visits his father today. Nelson currently resides on a palatial estate in upstate New York, at least until the owners of the palatial estate find out about it. He is married to a movie star and drives a Range Rover.

Christopher Pike

No one does it better than Christopher Pike. His mystery and suspense novels are so fast-paced and gripping that they're guaranteed to keep you on the edge of your seat, guessing whodunit...